Melody of a Curse

Janna Ruth

First published in New Zealand in 2022

www.janna-ruth.com

978-0-473-63891-7 (Paperback)

978-0-473-63892-4 (e-book)

For those who've lost their dreams.
May you find them again.

In front of you is a magical fairy tale full of dance and music. But every fairy tale has its dark origins, and this is no different. If you'd rather have no spoilers, skip this and enjoy. If you'd like to know what to expect, keep reading.

In *Melody of a Curse*, the main character is a veteran soldier, suffering from post-traumatic stress disorder (PTSD). The scenes around his war trauma may be upsetting if you've experienced similar trauma or know someone who has. There will be mention of blood and death, but it won't be in graphic detail. PTSD can be a severe affliction. It cannot be healed by love and magic, but therapy. The tale in front of you will reflect that, instead of romanticising mental health.

Themes of loss and grief will also be present in a less prominent fashion, as well as the use of alcohol, drugs (only suggested, not actual) and physical fighting. If any of these topics bear potential triggers for you, don't worry. Close the book and pick another from your TBR pile. Books should be enjoyed, not hurt us.

If you're happy to read on, welcome to The DeModie, the wondrous place of dreams and desires, and last stop of lost souls.

Love, Janna

Contents

Ouverture

Debris and ash were falling from the sky. Jonas threw himself flat on the ground. He had barely lain down when a second explosion shook the earth. Screams rose, mixed with the howls of sirens. Jonas pressed his hands to his ears, but just as merciless as the shards of glass, the screams drilled deep into his head. A wave of heat surged over him, bringing with it the smell of burning flesh. The screams grew louder, shrieks inhumanly high. He could not escape them; he burned with them and bled with them. At the same time, he dug himself out of the rubble, straining with all his strength, his head always down. *Keep your head down. Stay low.* If he could only get far enough away, he might stand a chance.

For the third time, his surroundings were torn to pieces.

It was his own scream that finally jolted Jonas out of his nightmares. Disoriented and gasping for breath, he looked around the small room. There was no shattered glass anywhere, the beams weren't broken and the man in the other bed wasn't gasping for air, but snoring. Jonas' heart was beating furiously, the sheets soaked with sweat, and tears were burning in his eyes. But he was safe.

Groaning, Jonas dropped back into the pillow and stared at the ceiling. The gruesome screams still echoed in his head, interrupted only by increasingly violent detonations. The soldier's life and war were behind him, yet, they wouldn't let him go. It was as if he was standing still while the world continued to spin without him. As if there was nothing else but this nightmare. The longer he stared at the ceiling, the more violently he felt the shocks as bombs kept exploding in his head.

The scar on his back hurt and Jonas couldn't stand it any longer. He flipped back the covers and got out of bed. A glance at the clock told him it was only four in the morning.

As he dressed, he listened to his surroundings. Apart from the snoring of his roommate, the hostel lay in complete silence. Even the group of bawling teenagers from the night before had long since gone to bed. It was this silence that invited the nightmares at night. The silence inside him that he was unable to dispel. Already, the memories he was trying to forget were creeping back in.

He was in desperate need of a change of scenery. Sounds. Life.

Jonas decided to leave the hostel and use the morning to familiarise himself with this new city. With a little luck, he would hold a job again, and would be able to build a new life for himself. All he had to do was get through the job interview without experiencing one of his fits.

The fresh air helped him clear away the remnants of his nightmares. It was pleasant outside, not as hot as during the day. The night was filled with sounds. A cooler dripped somewhere behind him, while crickets chirped in the grass. A rustling in the bushes caught Jonas' attention. There had been no bushes in the war, only cold bare stone.

The youth hostel was on a hill outside the tranquil little town where his interview would be. Jonas had to walk a bit until he had an unobscured view of the city. Most of the houses lay in darkness, the only light coming from the streetlights. Inevitably, his gaze was drawn to a small sea of lights to the south.

As if of their own accord, his feet carried Jonas towards company. Long before he reached the lit streets, he could hear the pulse of life. A bass boomed ahead, mingling with other rhythms, and soon enough, he could make out singular melodies. People staggered across the street, laughing and bawling. To his right, a young couple bickered at each other, while further ahead people sang along loudly and out of tune.

Relieved, he let the sounds carry him along.

The day was dawning when, next to Jonas, the door of a club opened. Laughter filled the air. A group of giggling girls stumbled out and joked with the bouncer. Their liveliness captivated Jonas, and he watched the cheerful revellers as they supported each other, chattering loudly and bursting into laughter every now and then.

One of the young women in particular caught Jonas' eye. Despite her intoxicated state, she pranced behind the others, as if listening to music only she could hear. As he looked at her, Jonas felt his lips form a smile for the first time in a long while.

It took him a while to notice that she was barefoot. Irritated, he followed her trail back and discovered the abandoned shoes near the club door. They weren't high heels, as he had expected, but pointe shoes, like the ones used in ballet. Jonas bent down to pick them up and hurried to catch up to the small group who had now hailed a taxi.

"Excuse me?" he called, and the girl turned to him expectantly. For a moment, Jonas lost himself in her dark eyes. Then he cleared his throat and lifted the shoes into the air. "You forgot something."

Wavering, she looked first to her bare toes, as if she needed to verify the accuracy of his statement. "Oh, right. Thank you."

Again, Jonas looked at the shoes in his hands. The soles and laces were worn, the straps frayed and dirty. "They seem to be a little worn out."

The girl looked up and laughed. "Yeah, kind of." As if she could never stand still long enough, she pranced around on the spot until she stumbled forward.

With his left hand, Jonas grabbed her arm. Heat spread through his stomach as he helped her regain her balance. "Are you alright?"

She nodded and brushed several strands from her face, an amused grin on her lips.

Clearing his throat, Jonas handed her the shoes. "Here."

Immediately, she raised her hands in defence. "Oh no! My feet already hurt like hell. I've been dancing all night. I don't think I could even tie my laces."

In her condition, Jonas believed her all too readily.

Still, he insisted on giving her the shoes. "Sure, but..."

"They're just shoes! Broken shoes!" The girl grinned mischievously, and Jonas couldn't help but do the same. "*You* keep them!" she suddenly suggested with exuberance.

The absurdity of her suggestion made Jonas snort. "I'm afraid they're too small for me." To his delight, her entire face brightened as she burst into laughter.

"Come on, Sophie! The taxi's waiting," one of her friends urged, holding the door open for her.

With a final grin, Sophie waved at him and stumbled into the taxi. The door slammed shut and the lively laughter faded away.

Sighing, Jonas looked after the taxi, the broken ballet slippers still in his hand. When the car turned a corner, he checked out the club.

DeModie.

The name was written in dark, twisted letters above a narrow, nondescript wooden door. The longer he looked, the more it seemed to merge with the building. If Jonas hadn't been standing right next to it earlier, he would've never spotted the entrance among the glowing neon signs of the neighbouring clubs.

Confused, Jonas turned away and continued walking, Sophie's image before his eyes. He was still smiling, and he felt more alive than he had in a long time. For once, in a good mood, he whistled a little song as the world around him slowly woke from its slumber.

"Interesting joint, isn't it?" a voice said from below.

It took Jonas a moment before he could make out the beggar in his pile of blankets. Nothing about the man was striking. His matted hair hung low on his face and his eyes darted around unsteadily. A worn plastic cup stood before him.

After a moment of hesitation, Jonas fumbled for his wallet and dropped a few coins into the cup. "What do you mean?"

The beggar grinned at him, baring crooked yellow teeth. "The DeModie. Every maiden's dream."

"Maiden?" repeated Jonas incredulously. The last time he had encountered that word, it had been in a storybook. He looked back to where The DeModie was literally disappearing among the other clubs. "Looks more like a hovel to me."

The man coughed and patted the ground beside him. "Exactly. It's not supposed to attract just anyone."

Jonas hesitated. The beggar wasn't exactly the company he'd been craving. But what if he wasn't the only one dying for a friendly chat? "So, whose attention is it supposed to draw?" he asked as he took a seat next to him. "Some kind maidens?"

The beggar's blue eyes twinkled in amusement as he reached forward and slipped the cup between his warm blankets. "You'll see, you'll see."

Jonas wondered what exactly he would see, but the man was preoccupied with himself and muttered, "Somewhere... I know it... yes, yes, time and its dreams... Ah, there you are."

Second-guessing his decision to sit down, Jonas was just about to get up, when the man took out a small bottle. Grunting, he poured the coins from his cup and filled it with a golden liquid, then held the cup out. "Here, drink!"

Doubtful, Jonas looked at the grey rim of the cup. His thoughts immediately jumped to the numerous bacteria that were surely cavorting within. He didn't even want to think about what illnesses he would contract from it.

And, so what?

If the war hadn't killed him, this cup certainly wouldn't. He reached for the cup and took a sip. He almost spat it out again. The liquor tasted disgusting.

Laughing, the beggar took the cup from him and emptied it in one go. "Not used to much, eh?"

Jonas screwed up his face, the disgusting taste still lingering on his tongue.

"But well-mannered and friendly. Not everyone sits down with old Manu."

"What kind of club is that?" Jonas asked when he could breathe again, trying to get at least something sensible out of the old man.

"Oh, the most beautiful place on Earth, richer than any treasury, and filled with heavenly pleasures." The man regarded the club longingly before turning away again. "And the coldest. Here, let me give you something."

To Jonas' dismay, the beggar began to peel off the topmost blanket, which turned out to be a ragged winter coat, and handed it to him.

Jonas raised his hands in protest. "Oh no, I can't accept that. You need it more than I do. It's still warm now, but later..."

"Take it, boy," the beggar growled, with surprising vehemence. "This is no ordinary coat."

Sceptically, Jonas raised his brows. "It isn't?"

The beggar nodded, his mind already elsewhere. "You will discover its secret yet. Believe me, it'll be more use to you than me. It's from the club."

"I..." Jonas could think of nothing to say in reply and left it at a simple, "Thank you."

The beggar smiled benevolently. "Trust me. You can use it to get to all of those wonderful dreams."

Jonas looked doubtfully at the tattered coat. Now he was the owner of not one but two items of clothing that belonged in the nearest bin. Maybe he should consider opening a second-hand shop when the job interview went south, as usual.

No sooner had the beggar handed over his gift, he lost interest. "Now get out of here, boy!"

Irritated, Jonas stood up. As he slowly backed away, he kept glancing over his shoulder. The beggar paid him no more attention and instead disappeared back into his blankets, as unassuming as The DeModie.

Jonas regarded his new heirloom. In the sunlight, it no longer looked so dirty. On the contrary, the dirt had disappeared, revealing a fabric finer than anything he had ever held. It felt incredibly light, and yet soft, like velvet. When he rubbed the fine fabric back and forth between his fingers, it even shimmered in the sunlight.

Seriously doubting his sanity, Jonas checked the shoes in his other hand, but they looked just as worn as before.

Jonas rubbed his eyes. Perhaps the sleep disruptions were leaving their mark after all. Casting one last doubtful look back, Jonas noticed that the corner was completely empty, as if the beggar had never been there. Shaking his head, he looked at the strange coat in his hand. The cut was old-fashioned and the fabric a good hand's breadth too long for him, although the old man hadn't seemed that tall.

He fervently hoped the rest of his day wouldn't be as confusing. After all, his future was at stake.

—

"So, what have you been doing for the last three years?"

The question corroded Jonas' guts. Nervously, he looked at the well-groomed man with thinning hair who sat in his imposing chair and regarded him critically. It was the analytical look Jonas knew from military officers, as if calculating the chances Jonas would survive the next mission.

Jonas cleared his throat and reached for the glass of water in front of him. It wasn't the first time. "I started studying." The details of those pathetic attempts were written in his CV.

"But?" The man had raised one of his bushy eyebrows and was tapping his fingers lightly on his desk.

Remembering his time in the army, Jonas straightened his spine and reported, "I started my studies too early and struggled with the transition." The nightmares had begun around that time. "This many people in one place made me uncomfortable, and so I stayed home more often than was conducive to my grade average. Another attempt was unsuccessful due to unexpected absences because of..." Gulping, he thought of the panic attacks that had tormented him then; days he had spent cowering under the bed. Days he had only experienced as dark episodes of his nightmare world.

The steely gaze of his counterpart made Jonas nervous. It was impossible for him to return it, so instead he glanced around the luxurious office. Retiring from active duty had worked well for Mr Kallenbach. The chairs in the large, bright office were upholstered in fine leather, and expensive paintings hung on the walls. When his eyes returned to the retired officer, he noticed he was still being watched closely.

Finally, Mr Kallenbach relieved him and said in a calm voice, "You brought back more from the war than you expected."

Jonas stared at his fingers. He was embarrassed the war had taken such a toll on him. He had fought bravely, carried out every mission, and returned home alive. That was more than some of his comrades could claim. What would they say now if they saw how he was afraid of even the slightest shaking of the ground, or that the memories tormented him every night? What would they think if they knew he was unable to enjoy life to the fullest? That he could no longer find his way back into that life?

Again, Jonas cleared his throat and nodded. "I'm doing my best."

They both knew "his best" was pitifully little. Nevertheless, Mr Kallenbach was willing to continue. "What does 'good work ethic' mean to you?"

"Diligence, attention to detail, both thinking on the spot and the willingness to carry out orders without question, reliability," Jonas enumerated, returning the gaze nonchalantly this time.

Mr Kallenbach nodded and leaned forward a little. "And are you that? Reliable?"

Self-consciously, Jonas slid around on the chair until the steely gaze forced him to regain his composure. "Yes, sir!" He almost saluted. Instead, he lowered his gaze. "I was awarded the Bronze Cross of Honour for my military service. Whatever task you have for me, you can count on me." The promise had slipped out of Jonas unexpectedly. He actually had no idea what Mr Kallenbach expected of him.

After several of his own attempts to rebuild life in this new reality, Jonas had told his former squad leader of his difficulties. Of course, he hadn't told him about the nightmares. Nor had he needed to. The truth had been clear for everyone to see in his eyes.

His squad leader had finally recommended him to Mr Kallenbach, who was in the process of hiring someone trustworthy.

"I'll be honest with you. I don't think you're suited for the job."

Jonas' heart sank. Things were starting to look dicey that he'd get anything out of his life and not end up in security or, worse, rubbish collection.

"But I'm the last person not to give a young man a chance."

Jonas perked up in surprise.

Mr Kallenbach leaned back. "I would like to hire you as my personal assistant. Your squad leader mentioned that you know something about logistics and administration."

Jonas nodded again. He had enjoyed working in the camp, even if he had only carried out orders.

Satisfied, Mr Kallenbach continued, "I take it you haven't found yourself permanent accommodation in this town, yet?"

This time, Jonas shook his head. It would have been next on his list.

"Fine. You can move into the guest flat on the other side of the estate. I will take care of the rest of the formalities. The salary will be equivalent to that of my security staff." With those words, he slid an envelope across the table to Jonas. At his nod, Jonas took it and glanced at the contract. When he saw the numbers, he felt dizzy. He couldn't afford to turn the job down.

"Your first assignment, however, will demand different qualities from you. Think of it as a test. It involves my daughter, Sophie," Mr Kallenbach explained.

Confused, Jonas reached for the glass of water, only to find that he had long since emptied it.

Without comment, Mr Kallenbach pushed the bottle over and continued speaking: "Every night she disappears and only reappears at daybreak. She neither tells me where she is going nor confides in anyone else. All attempts to follow her end with the same result. She always disappears off the face of the Earth. I've had the area where she disappears thoroughly searched, without success."

"Wouldn't that be something more suited to a private detective?" Jonas had only been a common soldier. He wouldn't even know where to start with the task.

Mr Kallenbach sighed. "Believe me, I've put several people on the task. I don't know why they all fail. You, however, are not much older than my daughter. Perhaps you can find out where she hangs out night after night."

Nervously, Jonas moistened his lips. He wasn't comfortable with the idea of shadowing the girl. Yet, he needed the money, and much more so, the chance. As he wrestled with himself, Mr Kallenbach gradually lost patience. "So, what's it going to be?"

"I'm not comfortable with such a task," Jonas admitted.

Before he could explain himself, however, Mr Kallenbach snorted, "If you do your job well, I'll write you a glowing recommendation that will get your foot into several doors. Or you can stay with the company, if that works for you."

Jonas knew he couldn't refuse the offer. Maybe there was another way to get the information. She might tell him if he explained the issue to her. Still, his lips were dry as he replied, "I'll do it. When do I start?"

A heavy duffel bag with all his belongings over his shoulder, Jonas approached the house on the edge of the Kallenbach estate. Compared to the office complex and the large mansion, the guest house was downright tiny. But it was secluded enough that he could pretend to live in his own little home instead of in his employer's estate.

Thinking about the job ahead, Jonas opened the door and immediately tripped over something. In front of him, chaos ruled.

The entrance led into a large living area that looked as if a bomb had hit it. Clothes, jackets, and shoes were scattered about, dirty dishes were piled up in the open kitchen, and at least a dozen different magazines—fashion, celebrities, and cultural events—were strewn across the table and the sofa. Everything in Jonas resisted the mess, and his hands twitched nervously with the desire to tidy up.

Unlike a bomb strike, however, this chaos was not one of death and destruction, but the result of living. The classical music that drifted from an adjoining room hit a similar vein. Surprised that he obviously wasn't the only occupant of the guesthouse, Jonas put his backpack down next to the door and went searching for the source of music.

He had expected anything, but certainly not a dance studio complete with barre and mirrored walls. On the opposite side were a piano and a state-of-the-art music system, and on the floor a girl was pirouetting, one leg raised high, toes and arms stretched. He recognised her by the way she planted her feet, light-footed and buoyant, long before he saw her face. It was the girl from last night, whose shoes he still had in his travel bag. Sophie.

In front of his eyes, she performed breath-taking leaps and pirouettes, every movement in sync with the music, as if she and the melody were one.

Jonas watched her, forgetting everything around him. He admired her elegance now that she was no longer drunk but wide awake and focused. Unlike last night, she had tied her dark blonde hair into a flawless bun. The only thing she wore was a skin-coloured bodysuit, which gave Jonas a far-too-detailed image of her body.

His face flushed, he was about to sneak out again, when Sophie froze in mid-motion, her eyes widening in shock. Instantly, Jonas realised how this must seem to her: a strange man standing in her dance hall, gawking at her.

Embarrassed, he held out his hand. "Jonas Grienkamp. I'm assuming you're Sophie. Your father hired me and gave me the keys to the house. I wasn't aware that you lived here."

As he spoke, he could see her brow crease in annoyance. She crossed her arms in front of her chest. "That probably slipped his mind, didn't it?" Rolling her eyes, she unfolded her arms and pushed her hands into her hips. "Let me guess. You were hired to spy on me."

Surprised, Jonas widened his eyes. "I really didn't know the house was occupied. If I had known, I would have refused the offer."

"Well, you're here now," Sophie said, waving it off.

"I'll be gone in a minute. Really, I'm sorry I scared you." Slowly, Jonas took a few steps backwards. "But you dance really well. I mean... not that I wanted to watch you or anything. I..." Struck by nerves, Jonas interrupted his word vomit.

Sophie had followed his steps and started to smile. "Now don't get your knickers in a twist. You caught me dancing, not in the shower."

Jonas felt the blush creep up his face again.

"My dad obviously wants you to live nearby, and he gave you the keys. He's probably hoping that I'll immediately pack my bags screaming and return to the house, but that's not going to work. If he's decided I could handle a flatmate, then that's what we'll do." She was standing close to him now. Her dark eyes twinkled with amusement. "Unless you object."

"I uh..." His mouth had gone terribly dry. At last, Jonas shook his head.

Sophie laughed and reached for the towel hanging by the door. "There's just one little problem." As she rubbed her neck, she looked back at him. "I've claimed quite a bit of the flat. We'd have to clear the second bedroom first."

Jonas breathed a sigh of relief. He had been expecting the worst. "I can manage that," he replied, slowly relaxing a little.

"Great!" Sophie hung the towel back on its hook and untied her bun, letting her long hair fall down her back, as it had the night before.

Apparently, he seemed to be the only one who remembered their encounter. "Last night..."

Her eyes wide, Sophie turned to him. "So, you are a snitch after all!" Before Jonas could explain himself, she sighed and finally regarded him reproachfully. "That's your game plan? You're just going to ask me straight out what I did last night?"

"No, I already know where you were," Jonas explained. He was relieved, realising he didn't have to spy on her at all. "You visited The DeModie. That little club on Niemeyer Street."

Her eyes grew wide with surprise. "You've been to The DeModie before?"

With a slight shake of his head, Jonas replied, "No, I was there when you came out. Don't you remember? We were talking to each other. I was... Wait."

Curious, Sophie followed him back to the entrance to where his bag was and threw on a cardigan she grabbed from the back of the armchair.

It didn't take long for Jonas to find the shoes wrapped in the strange coat. With a wry smile, he handed them to her.

"Oh, my... My shoes! How did you get them?" she exclaimed, beaming with joy.

Caught off guard by her overwhelming joy over the broken shoes, Jonas rubbed the back of his neck. "Well, like I said. I saw you last night, and you had left them outside the club. When I tried to give them back to you, you offered them to me. Or something like that."

Now Sophie was blushing. "Oh man, that's so embarrassing. I guess I was pretty hammered. I woke up earlier and couldn't remember what had happened at all. I thought I'd lost them forever." She took the tattered shoes with near reverence.

Touched, she looked up at Jonas, then suddenly took a step forward and breathed a kiss onto his cheek. "Thank you."

Caught by surprise, Jonas could only grin stupidly in return. Maybe this job wasn't that bad after all.

—

"What is it about The DeModie that makes everyone act so secretively?" Jonas asked as he carried the next box of Sophie's stuff out of the small bedroom. Sophie hadn't lied when she'd said it needed clearing. But slowly, the bed in the room could be glimpsed. With luck, he would even find some closet space by evening.

Sophie was rummaging through the scattered things in the living room, holding an outfit up to the mirror now and then. "Oh, it's a dance club. It's pretty exclusive, so they don't let just anyone in."

Which apparently meant they wouldn't let him in. "And what's so special about it?" He set the box down on the sofa and watched her turn back and forth in front of the mirror.

She turned and looked curiously into the box in front of him. "Oh, it's exquisite. Very expensive, select guests, the best music in the whole city." Sophie reached for something golden from the box. "There you are!"

Never in a million years would Jonas have mistaken the piece of fabric for a dress, but Sophie took it out, pressed it coquettishly against her body, and then ran to her room. "Be right back," she called, before the door slammed shut.

Jonas shook his head with a grin and continued his task. He was surprisingly glad Sophie agreed to live with him. Her cheerful chatter and bell-bright laughter had already made his day.

"Will you give me a hand?" When Sophie returned, she had put on the skimpy dress. She turned her back to him. "Can you zip me up?"

The view of her bare back stirred something in Jonas he had long forgotten.

The dress, if it could even be called that, was far too short. Golden ruffles sat above her hips, not nearly long enough to pass for a skirt. It was more of a dance costume, but Sophie moved as naturally in it as if she had just slipped into comfort clothes.

Trying not to stare too hard or touch her accidentally in the process, he pulled up the zip.

"Thank you so much."

"You're welcome," Jonas muttered, watching her prance off again and into the bathroom.

The door wide open, Sophie began to apply make-up. "If you're hungry, check the fridge. I think there's some broccoli and beans somewhere," she babbled cheerfully. "You're welcome to cook yourself something. I haven't got around to shopping this week." Sophie was rushing past him again, looking for something else. "You don't have to wait up for me, though."

"Because you're going to stay out all night?" asked Jonas, catching himself watching her.

Sophie turned to him with a curling iron in her hand, beaming. "That's right. I'll be back here by sunrise."

At her smile, a tingle spread through Jonas' stomach. Forcibly grumpy so as not to give anything away, Jonas murmured, "I'll be asleep then."

She just smirked and vanished into the bathroom once more.

Jonas sighed. Sophie's zest for life filled him with a confidence and hope he hadn't known for a long time. Her laugh was truly magical.

"How do I look?" Her question snapped him out of his thoughts. Sophie pirouetted in front of him, sending the ruffles on her dress flying.

"Er... good. Great. I mean... very, very nice," Jonas stammered, feeling like a fool.

Amused, Sophie giggled and made her way to the door. "Well, here we go, then." To his surprise, however, she didn't choose high heels that would have matched the sexy look. Instead, she reached for last night's worn pointe shoes.

Irritated, Jonas watched her tie the laces. He had never seen anyone wear pointe shoes to go out. Though at least that explained their desolate state.

Sophie straightened up. "Enjoy your first night!" she said with a grin and opened the door. "See you in the morning."

The door slammed shut, and all at once, silence fell. No rustling, no excited chatter, and certainly no laughter. Without Sophie, the little house seemed much emptier and more sinister. There were shadows he hadn't noticed before. Jonas regarded the door anxiously. It would be far too easy for someone to kick it open.

What had he been thinking, taking this job? Or letting Sophie talk him into the flat share? That hadn't worked out in the dormitory at the university. His nightmares had never remained hidden from the others for long, and the need to explain had driven him out of the house.

Jonas' gaze darted nervously around the room. He was certain the walls would not withstand a grenade attack. Suddenly, it seemed impossible for him to spend a night in this strange house. His breathing quickened. With great difficulty, he managed to force himself to sit down and take a deep breath.

He was in Germany. No one would attack tonight, he kept telling himself, while he kept his hands busy unpacking. The house was safe. Still, Jonas' hands shook more by the minute.

Maybe it would be better if he took another look at The DeModie. Not to spy on Sophie, but because the club made him curious. His fingers felt the soft fabric of the old coat he had received from the beggar, and his mind was made up.

If Jonas hadn't known exactly where The DeModie had been the previous night, he wouldn't have found it again. The dark club was squeezed so tightly between the busy neighbouring bars that Jonas wondered how there was even room for a dance hall worth mentioning. For most of the nightly revellers, who were slowly arriving, the entrance was invisible. Only now and then did a group purposefully find its way in and gain immediate entry.

Jonas finally decided to try his luck and knocked on the door. Nothing happened. No music even filtered through the metal out to him on the street, though he could clearly hear the competing beats of neighbouring clubs. He spent ten minutes waiting before a group of young people approached, and the door began to open. Had he bypassed a motion detector?

The surprisingly young and handsome bouncer who opened the door looked at him first with irritation, then with unkindness. "Get out of here, man! You don't belong here."

"And why's that?" asked Jonas, irritably. He'd never had the nerve for childish power games. The bouncer crossed his arms, and Jonas sighed heavily. "What appears to be the problem?"

While blocking his way, the bouncer didn't even glance at the three teenagers as they slipped past them. "We don't let guys like you in here."

The answer left Jonas speechless. Before he could reply, the door had already closed again. Guys like him? Jonas didn't know what to make of that. He knew bouncers liked to assert their power or make their decision based on absurd things like choice of clothing; he hadn't dressed up like Sophie and was only wearing a plain shirt and trousers. But then again, the three teenagers hadn't looked like they came from money either.

Sighing, Jonas glanced at the reflective glass of the neighbouring club and startled. Deep circles lay under his eyes, and he was pale. It had been a while since he had last seen himself in the mirror, but the fact that he looked so sickly frightened him. When had he let himself go? No wonder they wouldn't let him into the club.

Still, he was suddenly determined to find a way in. The curiosity was killing him. Maybe it would be enough if he wore the strange coat he had received from the beggar. It was noble enough, after all, despite the dreadful style.

Jonas decided that, apart from his dignity, he had nothing to lose by dressing in such an old-fashioned piece, and threw the coat around himself. Instinctively, he also put up the hood, though the temperatures didn't demand it. He didn't know much about fashion, but even he realised he looked down-right ridiculous. Inwardly, Jonas was preparing himself for the bouncer's ridicule.

He was about to knock when he was suddenly jostled from behind. Without so much as muttering an apology, the two young women looked straight through him and smiled bright-ly. Irritated, Jonas turned around and discovered the door of The DeModie was open again. The doorman smiled kind-ly, almost charmingly, and bowed elegantly. "Good evening, ladies." He ignored Jonas completely.

In the face of such disparagement, anger crept up inside of Jonas. To deny him entry had been one thing, but to act as if he were nothing but air was too much. With all the self-confidence he could still find in himself, Jonas straightened his back and went after the giggling women, not even glancing at the bouncer. At any moment, he expected to be grabbed by the arm and pulled backwards, but the bouncer closed the door behind him without a comment. Perhaps the coat was some kind of secret symbol that he belonged.

Darkness enveloped him, and it took a moment for his eyes to adjust. After a while, Jonas spotted a faint glow in the corridor and began to feel his way down. Steps. The club was below the others, hence the narrow entrance. Ahead of him, he could hear the two women whispering excitedly. Silently, so as not to give himself away, he followed them.

The sight that met his eyes when he finally turned the corner almost took his breath away. Instead of a crowded narrow club, a forest of gold and silver trees stretched out ahead of and below him, shining so magnificently his eyes began to water. A gentle breeze made the filigree leaves tinkle in a delightful melody.

The stairs led straight through the seemingly endless forest. Jonas looked up at the ceiling, but from what source the unreal light came from that made the forest glitter and sparkle, he could not discover. Instead, dark billows of clouds piled up on the ceiling. "Smoke effects," Jonas whispered, only then noticing that his unwilling companions were already halfway down the stairs. Hastily, he followed them so he wouldn't lose them. Who knew whether The DeModie had any other obstacles in store for him?

The two women were not in the least disturbed by his presence. They dreamily raved about the handsome men they were about to meet. Even when one glanced briefly over her shoulder, her gaze went straight through Jonas. Then he remembered. The old man had talked about the cloak having a secret. Was he actually invisible?

Jonas raised his hand to check his insane thought, but it still looked exactly the same. Invisible! It was more likely that the two women were simply not interested in someone else entering the club behind them.

Shaking his head, he continued walking. Again and again, his gaze slipped to the magnificent decorations and discovered detail after detail. What he had thought were leaves on a silver branch turned out to be a swarm of butterflies with metallic wings. As they rose into the air, new leaves sprouted from the bare branch. A golden-winged hummingbird buzzed from flower to flower, sucking their nectar. Where the nectar dripped onto the ground, new filigree webs formed. They were so delicate that they gave way under the lightest touch of Jonas' fingertips.

It was only when he had almost reached the bottom of the stairs that he noticed the unusual music blending seamlessly with the melodic tinkling of leaves. The sounds were almost ethereal, but each note struck a different chord in him, setting his nerves vibrating. The bass rumbled in his stomach and he could barely fight the urge to sway along.

While he wondered which artist he had been missing all these years, the forest opened up to reveal a subterranean lake that took up almost the entire room.

Jonas froze. "Someone pinch me," he whispered in the face of the overwhelming dimensions and detail. On the shore, pebbles shimmered in a wide variety of colours, and as Jonas bent down and let them trickle through his fingers, he remarked in amazement at how heavy they were.

"The riches of The DeModie..." Astonished, he rose. He was almost giddy at the thought of how much the interior design might have cost. The cave alone was an architectural masterpiece. The expensive decorations and impressive special effects were just the icing on the cake.

At least that's what Jonas thought until he spotted the shiny black castle on the other shore. Certain that he had now gone completely mad, he rubbed his eyes and looked again. The castle was still there. Imposing and powerful, it rose beyond the lake, almost as if the ground above it didn't exist.

Jonas stood dumbfounded for several minutes, unable to take his eyes off the battlements. His thoughts stumbled from a cost estimate to the logistical challenges to the physical principles that tried to apply some logic to what he was seeing.

It was only when a laughing couple almost bumped into him that he noticed the dancers gliding weightlessly across the pond, and realised he'd fallen victim to an optical illusion. What he had perceived as water was actually a mirror-smooth dance floor on which the visitors swirled. Small boats were crafted into seating areas. The castle, on the other hand, was merely part of the masterfully designed back wall where the bar and mixer were located.

Jonas exhaled with relief. This exclusive club might indeed hold unspeakable riches, but he had not accidentally descended into another world or lost his mind. Everyone was looking through him as he mingled with the dancers, giving him goosebumps. His mind could not accept that he was truly invisible, but he had to get used to the idea, because even when Jonas took a glass of beer straight from a waiter's tray, the man only stared into space.

Overwhelmed, he leaned against the castle wall, which was actually made of black stone, or at least a very good imitation. The beer calmed his nerves, and he let his eyes wander through the crowd again. He wondered who owned the club and what the beggar and his strange coat had to do with it. But then he saw what he had been looking for, and at the same moment, a bitter taste spread through his mouth.

Sophie was not far from him in the arms of a man he could only describe with one word: gorgeous. The stranger looked like a young god: well-defined muscles, a sharply cut face, blue eyes, and blond, coiffed hair. As if that wasn't enough, he was also an exquisite dancer, deftly and elegantly leading Sophie across the dance floor.

The worst thing, however, was how Sophie looked at him. It was as if her dance partner was all that existed in her world, that enamoured was she. So, that was the whole mystery behind Sophie's nightly disappearance. She had a lover with whom she spent every single night and wanted to keep secret from her father.

The thought left a stale taste on Jonas' tongue that not even the beer could wash away. For a while, he couldn't take his eyes off the two as the strange dancer spun Sophie in endless pirouettes, sending her golden ruffles flying, and lifted her high into the air. But it was Sophie who fascinated Jonas, with the exquisite shapes her body formed when she threw her legs in the air or her arched back in the man's arms, like a young willow. The excitement was written on her flushed face. Watching her, Jonas could almost believe that she enjoyed the dance more than the presence of her immaculate partner.

At least until the music ended and Sophie fell into her lover's arms, laughing, and they shared a passionate kiss. Disappointed, Jonas pushed himself off the wall, placed the empty glass on the nearest table and pushed his way across the dance floor towards the exit. Suddenly, all the over-the-top luxury disgusted him.

He was halfway up the stairs when he remembered his mission. If he was going to report to her father, he needed proof of the whimsical club. Sophie certainly wouldn't back up his words and who knew if the coat would let him in another time. Instead, Jonas' gaze lingered on the silver branches. The club had so many of them that it probably wouldn't even be noticed. Bravely, Jonas stepped forward and snapped one off.

Instantly, a crash sounded, so loud it was as if the walls around him were collapsing. The ground shook and dust burned in his lungs.

The war had caught up to him.

Cavalier

The music came to a sudden stop, causing Sophie to stumble. She turned around in confusion and saw the worried faces of the people around them. The silence crept into her limbs, and she suddenly felt terribly cold. Even the lighting in The DeModie was a little dimmer, as if some of the lamps high up in the clouds had burnt through. Before Sophie could mention it, the music began once more. Unlike before, it sounded slightly out of tune in the most unpleasant way, as if there was a scratch on the record. Nevertheless, the people next to her started dancing like there was nothing out of the ordinary. It only made the whole experience weirder.

"What was that?" whispered Sophie, pressing herself against Luca's chest.

Luca's strong arms wrapped around her and held her tight. "Bastien probably turned the base up too loud and caused a short circuit. Hey, Tomas," he called, taking a few steps towards the passing waiter.

While the two were talking, Sophie spotted a red welt on Luca's neck. Guilt washed over her. She hadn't even noticed that she had scratched him in her exuberance. Or had it happened when that terrible thunder crashed? The uneasy feeling was still there, as if someone was watching her.

At last, Luca came back with a wry smile while Tomas hurried away. "He's going to check if everything's okay."

"Great. Uhm, do you feel like everyone is suddenly staring at us?" The words seemed silly as soon as they'd left her mouth.

Luca pulled her close with a smirk. "If they're staring at you, it's because you're so beautiful." His kiss on her lips almost made her forget her misgivings.

When he led her back into the dance, the music didn't even sound that off anymore, but Sophie couldn't shake the feeling. People were definitely watching her.

"Does that person have horns?" she asked, startled, but realised in an instant it was just their hair in a high ponytail. Suddenly tired, Sophie rubbed her eyes.

"What do you mean?" Was she mistaken, or did Luca sound tense?

With some effort, she tore her gaze from the others and looked back at him. "I think I need a break. I'm starting to see things that aren't there. Shall we have something to drink?"

Something weird was going on in Luca's gaze, but then he shook his head and his usual smile returned. "Of course, come with me. I've got the boat reserved in the back." Sophie's heart skipped a beat at the prospect of being alone with Luca. Usually, they sat with her friends.

No sooner had they taken their seats than Tomas came over and served them his bright blue signature drink. As he did so, he leaned in to tell Luca, "Nothing. I don't know what happened there. Bastien and I checked everything but found nothing."

Luca frowned, but nodded. "I'll take another look later. Thanks."

"Is everything all right?" asked Sophie, following Tomas with her eyes. When he had disappeared into the crowd, she turned back to Luca.

The latter put his arm around her and handed her the glass. "Yeah, sure, it'll be okay. Probably someone tripped against the stereo or something. Anyway, I'm not going to let that spoil a nice evening with you." With a smile, he leaned forward and toasted her.

His bright blue eyes sparkled, and Sophie couldn't help but kiss him before she took a sip. The delicious drink settled her nerves, and soon she was back to her usual chattiness. "Oh, that reminds me, I haven't told you that I almost lost my shoes. I'd taken them off outside the club and then just left them there." Luca frowned and Sophie hurried to say, "Don't worry. They miraculously found their way back to me." Grinning, she took another sip. As usual, Tomas had prepared it perfectly to her taste.

Luca grinned. "Is that so?" His hand stroked her back affectionately and Sophie slid a little closer.

Laughing, she nodded. "Yes!" She kissed him again, and for a while she was able to forget the club around her.

When she opened her eyes again, however, she had a terrible fright. In the neighbouring boat, thick fur covered the face of a man enjoying the company of two women. His yellow eyes glanced at Sophie. Her breathing quickened, and she hastily avoided his unpleasant gaze.

Luca's hot breath brushed her neck and seconds later Sophie felt his soft lips on her skin. For weeks, she had wanted nothing more, but the thought of what she had just seen stuck with her.

Cautiously, she cast another glance. The man in the neighbouring boat had already turned his attention back to his companions. There was no trace of fur. Instead, an impressive beard and bushy eyebrows adorned his face. He was probably just wearing yellow contact lenses to make himself seem more interesting.

Sophie sighed in relief and was about to turn back to Luca, who was still caressing her neck, when her glance fell on the hands of the two women. They were stroking their companion's muscular arms with long claws. Gasping, Sophie raised her hand to her mouth and subsequently spilled some of Tomas' drink on her bare legs.

"Hey, Sophie. What's wrong with you today?" Luca sounded irritated.

She realised that she had completely ignored his efforts and blushed. "Fingernails," Sophie breathed, certain that the women were simply wearing very long and pointy filed artificial fingernails. She shuddered.

"Is everything all right?" This time, she heard the concern in his words.

With some effort, she turned to Luca and nervously brushed a strand of hair from her face. "I think I've had too much to drink or something. I'm imagining all sorts of things that can't be there. Claws, horns, teeth." She rubbed her forehead. "It's crazy, right? I should probably go home."

Instead of the laugh she expected, Luca sighed and took his arm away.

Nervously, Sophie clutched her drink and silently scolded herself for her stupidity. At long last Luca had been willing to get more physical, and she was turning him off with her silliness.

For a while, Luca regarded her silently, as if searching for the right words. Finally, he raised a hand to stroke her cheek gently with his fingers. A little smile graced his lips, but his eyes still looked sombre, perhaps even sad. Sophie swallowed.

"I wanted to spare you, but I realise that wouldn't be fair," he finally whispered.

"What's not fair?" Sophie braced herself for the worst. She had known right away that it couldn't last forever. Luca was just too perfect: incredibly handsome, kind, loving, charming, and a stunning dancer. The fact that he had danced with her every night for three months was already more than Sophie could have ever dreamed of. If he broke up with her today, it would be entirely her fault.

The thought turned her stomach into knots as he continued, "For dragging you into this." Was there a hint of guilt in his gaze? "You should be able to dance the night away and not worry about me or feel obligated to me in any way."

Obviously, whatever it was that was bothering him was something more serious. The knot inside her dissolved, but her hands trembled. "Tell me what it is, already! Are you sick? Do you have to leave town, or will you be kicked out of the club?" Why couldn't he just tell it to her straight?

An unexpected glimmer of hope entered Luca's eyes. "I wish, Sophie. It's just that I... Even if I wanted to, I couldn't leave. I'm trapped here."

"Trapped?" Irritated, Sophie leaned back. "What's that supposed to mean? This isn't a prison, is it?"

There was no mirth in Luca's face now.

Nervously, Sophie shrugged and put down her glass. "So, tell me, who's holding you prisoner? Bastien? He just doesn't want to put on the music without you."

Luca didn't laugh at her joke. On the contrary, he lowered his head like a kicked dog, and Sophie immediately felt sorry for her careless words.

At last, he answered quietly, "The music."

Surprised, Sophie held her breath.

"This is no ordinary club, Sophie. In fact, it's only for people like you. For me and Bastien, Tomas and the others, it's more like... a home. We can't leave The DeModie." There was so much pain in his gaze that it startled her. Struggling to maintain some composure, Luca added with a shrug, "We'll probably never see a ray of sunlight in our lives."

The sentence was so absurd that Sophie could only shake her head in confusion. "I don't understand what you're trying to tell me. Is this some ploy to get rid of me?"

"No!" Luca's eyes widened in horror, and he grabbed her hands quickly. "Sophie, I would never want to get rid of you. On the contrary, I want to dance with you for the rest of my life."

Her heart leapt with joy, but Sophie couldn't let the emotions carry her away from the meaning. "So then answer me: what's so terribly unusual about this club, other than that it's obscenely big and rich? And how the hell are you held captive by the music? I mean, I often get lost in the music, too, but it's never stopped me from leaving the room before."

Luca sighed. "I understand that you have questions, and I want to try to answer them for you. But it's not that easy." He stroked her hands, lost in thought for a moment. When he looked up again, there was something bitter in his gaze. "The DeModie is nothing but the underworld. A wondrous place of dreams and desires, and last stop of lost souls."

Sophie stared at Luca for half an eternity, not knowing what to say or believe. But looking around her, there was a hint of melancholy in all the splendour. The music had returned to its usual intensity and the dance floor was full again. Her friends were having a great time, laughing and snuggling up to young men who had asked them to dance. But more people than before preferred to huddle in the shadows of the castle and gaze longingly at the dancers. There was something in their faces that Sophie could only describe with one word.

Hunger.

Luca's words snapped her out of her daze. "We're all cursed, Sophie, bound to this place forever." His voice sounded more insistent with each word.

Again, Sophie frowned. "And who cursed you?" She was finding it increasingly difficult to find enthusiasm for this conversation. Something was wrong with this club. Sophie got that much. Still, Luca's hare-brained attempts at explanation made her hair stand on end.

"In the case of me and my brothers, it was a sorceress," Luca replied, tenderly rubbing his thumb over Sophie's hand.

The loving touch was the only thing stopping Sophie from getting up and leaving. Instead, she tried to run with it a little longer. "Which brothers?"

"Well, Bastien, Tomas, and the others. I know I said we were just friends, but we're brothers. Twelve to be exact. Quite a lot, eh?"

"Your poor mother."

A cautious smirk flitted across Luca's face. "She had enough wet nurses. Besides, that's how it was back then."

"Wet nurses? Back then?" repeated Sophie. She really wanted to believe him, but it all sounded too far-fetched.

"I told you we were cursed." As if Luca had noticed that she doubted his words, he began to elaborate. "There was this sorceress, butthurt that none of us wanted to dance with her at the ball, and that..." Ashamed, Luca looked away. "My brothers and I were haughty. We were young and of royal lineage."

Sophie raised her eyebrows in disbelief.

"We thought we owned the world, and if we wanted to get married, all we had to do was snap our fingers and the girls would start queuing up. After all, they always had."

With his looks, Sophie wasn't the least bit surprised about *that* part.

"So, we danced with a different one every night and left a string of broken hearts behind." There was so much regret in his voice, Sophie couldn't bear to meet his eyes.

Quietly, Luca continued, "One day, there she was. An old, wizened hag that none of us would tolerate in our dance hall, let alone dance with." His voice turned bitter, and it seemed to cost him greatly to continue speaking. "So, she cursed us, snatched us from our family and brought us here to The DeModie. Only when we succeed in dancing with a girl for every night of a year and a day shall the curse be lifted." Again, he lowered his eyes. "So far, only Immanuel has managed to escape The DeModie."

He looked at her expectantly, and Sophie almost felt for him. Nevertheless, she was perfectly capable of taking the piss out of herself without his help. "Are you serious?"

The hope in Luca's gaze turned to despair. "Sophie, please. I know it sounds implausible, but I swear to you on my honour that I would never lie to you."

"Sure, you're a prince and a witch cursed you. And now a turntable is tying you to a luxury club." Sophie abruptly pulled her hands away and rose. "I don't get why you feel the need to tell me such fairy tales." Disappointed, she turned away.

She didn't get farther than three steps when Luca hugged her from behind and forced her to a halt. "Watch!" Gently, he lifted her chin so that her gaze fell on the glorious glittering forest. "And listen!"

Even though they were standing so far away, she could hear the delicate tinkling of leaves as they touched each other. A flock of butterflies rose, and the harmony of the leaves swinging back brought tears to Sophie's eyes. Only now did she realise that the bell-bright notes were part of the music playing around her. They set the beat and accents that made Sophie's heart beat faster.

Her feet called her to the dance floor, so that she might echo the music with her body. It was this longing to lose herself completely in the melody that carried Sophie into The DeModie night after night, and of course Luca, who guided her through complex moves without ever having practised them. As if there was no other way to dance.

She felt as if the rest of The DeModie was disappearing. Only she, Luca, and the magical music of the forest existed. Sophie flowed from one shape into another. The notes were so fragile her eyes filled with tears. She had never danced this slowly with Luca, given herself to him so completely. His arms held Sophie when she sought his closeness and released her when the music called her.

There was a depth to it that Sophie felt more with every step. She felt as if she were standing on the shore of an unfathomable lake and had just dipped her toe into the water. She could spend a lifetime here and not get tired of the melody.

But there was also something incongruous. A note that didn't harmonise with the others. A disturbance on the perfect surface. It was this tiny dissonance that finally broke the spell of the music and brought Sophie's feet to a stop.

With a wistful sigh, she turned to Luca. "That... that was wonderful."

Her joy died at the sight of the pain in Luca's eyes. "A place of wonder and longing," he agreed. "As intoxicating as the music is, it becomes a nuisance when it dictates your every move. I want to be out in the world again. To feel fresh air on my skin, to be dazzled by the bright light of the sun, and to be free. Free to do whatever I want or to do nothing at all."

As before with the music, Sophie lost herself in the tragedy of his words.

"Oh, Sophie." Luca leaned over and brushed the tears from her cheeks she hadn't even been aware of. "I really didn't mean to drag you into this." The next words took considerable effort on his part. "You're still free to go. I'm not going to stop you. After all, I know it's too much to ask."

"All I have to do," Sophie said carefully, "is dance with you every night for a whole year?"

With a sad smile, Luca nodded. "A year and a day." Carefully, he added, "That is, if you want to try. We're three months in already."

Tentatively, Sophie nodded, then smiled. "I can think of worse things than dancing with you every night."

Luca took her face in both hands and kissed her so passionately it felt as if the butterflies from the enchanted forest were flying in her stomach.

Humming happily to herself, Sophie reached home about dawn. She was still reminiscing about the last dance and bittersweet goodbye to Luca. She didn't like having to leave him behind now that she knew he couldn't follow her. She still couldn't quite believe the story of the curse, but she no longer had any doubts about his imprisonment. The longing look with which he had seen her off at the stairs couldn't be faked easily.

Sophie dreamily leaned back against her front door and looked up at the purplish clouds. What if it had been fate that had brought her and Luca together?

A sudden noise behind the door pulled Sophie out of her dreams. Hastily, she turned around, regarding the door with a pounding heart. It was so quiet she wasn't entirely sure she hadn't imagined the noise. She'd already seen a lot of strange things tonight, and she was slightly intoxicated by the music and the alcohol. No wonder she was beginning to let her imagination run away with her.

Still, she hesitated with her key. What if someone was in her house after all? Her mobile phone lay forgotten on the dresser inside, as usual, so calling for help was out of the question. She glanced at the villa behind the guest house. Her father would be pleased to assure her safety.

"Don't be such a scaredy-cat. There's no one there," she said to herself, though her heart was beating in her throat.

Shouldn't she go over to the villa, after all?

And admit to her father that she couldn't manage on her own? Never! Only now did Sophie notice how much her feet hurt. She had danced all night and was exhausted. Determined, she shook her head and put the key in the lock. She wouldn't let some random noise keep her from bed, would she?

"Come on." Despite her shaky hands, Sophie managed to unlock the door. She took a deep breath and gave the door a gentle push.

The door swung inwards, revealing an unparalleled chaos in the dim light. Sophie had never bothered keeping things tidy, but now half her furniture was turned upside down. Her things were scattered all over the room, and she spotted at least one broken vase. All at once, her stomach felt terribly queasy, and she wished she had run to her father after all. Tentatively, she called into the room instead: "Hello?"

No answer. Whoever had done this might have already been long gone.

Not far from her, Sophie saw her mobile phone. As quietly as possible, she crept over to the dresser. Her pulse was throbbing in her temple, and her hands felt damp and clammy. Sophie licked her dry lips and checked the display.

"I'm sorry."

Sophie flinched so violently the phone fell out of her hand, and she stumbled three steps backwards. With wide eyes, she looked at the half-dressed man who was now rising from behind the overturned armchair.

It was only when he stepped into the light that Sophie suddenly recognised him. "Oh, it's you." Right. There was the new roommate her father had burdened her with.

Some of the tension fell away, but the shock still ran too deep. As he came closer, Sophie quickly picked up her phone and held out a hand in a feeble attempt to protect herself. "Stay away from me!"

Fear flashed across Jonas' face. He stammered something unintelligible, stopped, and held on to the dining table as if his life depended on it. His voice sounded pitiful. "Sophie, I can explain."

Her pulse was calming, making way for more hostile feelings. "Give me one good reason why I shouldn't call the police."

Instead of answering her, Jonas' shoulders slumped. His face was contorted with suffering, and Sophie thought she saw alternating shame, fear, and pain in his eyes. His gaze no longer held hers, instead darting restlessly around the room, taking in the extent of the devastation.

"Have you been drinking?" Sophie demanded to know, not making good on her threat yet.

"No," he replied curtly, and Sophie eyed him more closely. His brown hair was tangled and there were deep, dark shadows under his eyes, but the way he held himself didn't look like he'd had a drink.

Sophie brushed a few strands from her face, not knowing what to do. "Are you sleepwalking?"

Jonas looked at her and swallowed. "No. Not really, anyway." Ashamed, he stared at the floor again. "It was just a... nightmare." The last word was barely audible.

Sophie exhaled and looked around the flat. The queasy feeling in her stomach wouldn't go away. She began to chatter, hoping it would help. "I thought you were a burglar or something. Not like there's much to steal here, but..." It didn't work as usual—her heartbeat was fluttering too much. She took a deep breath. "Your nightmares are pretty intense. Do you have them often?" She didn't want to imagine what else he could do in his sleep. "I... well..." She ran out of words when there was nothing but silence in his face. Jonas had gone terribly pale. His fingers clenched around the dining table as he kept trying to wet his lips with his tongue. Sophie feared he'd throw up any minute. "Should I call a doctor?" Again, she raised the mobile phone.

"Please don't," Jonas begged with a croak. "I'm sorry. I didn't think... I haven't had such a violent seizure in a long time. If I'd known, I never would have moved in here." He whispered the last sentence with his eyes closed. A heavy sigh followed. When he opened his eyes again, all he could utter was an exasperated, "Shit."

Panicked that he would get angry again, Sophie tried to distract him. "Don't worry about it. It was only a nightmare. We all have nightmares from time to time." Though that didn't mean they all tore the place apart in their sleep, she thought to herself. Her own words felt meaningless and flat to her.

"Only?" asked Jonas. The desperation in his voice tightened her chest. "I have nightmares every night."

The words stood between them like a wall. Neither knew what to say. Instead, they looked at each other until Sophie avoided his gaze and he lowered his head. As she took in the devastation one more time, she asked, "This happens every night?" There was no way he could stay, whether her father wanted him to or not.

"No, I usually wake up and keep it all in." He sounded weary. "I don't know why today was so intense. I... It was suddenly all so real. Like I was back there."

Jonas had sounded nonchalant, but Sophie couldn't help noticing how his shoulders slumped again. Since she couldn't think of a reason by herself, she finally asked him, "Where is there?"

"Afghanistan." He looked up and shrugged as if it was no big deal. Sophie knew this defence mechanism only too well. It helped keep the things she couldn't deal with at a distance.

"You were in the war?" It explained where her father had found someone like Jonas.

Jonas nodded mechanically and his voice was far steadier than before when he replied, "I served five years in the Bundeswehr. But it feels much longer."

Silence spread again as Sophie tried to make sense of all the information. As far as she knew, her father had never been involved in combat during his service. And if he had, he'd never told her about it. He'd certainly never dismantled their house. Jonas must've experienced far worse. Unwillingly, the images from the news came to her mind. It had all been so far away then, but somehow the war had managed to find them here in her living room.

Several times, Sophie opened her mouth, but no words came from her lips. Jonas was still holding onto the table like a drowning man clinging to a wooden beam. She was rarely at a loss for words, but this was a subject she didn't know how to approach. Finally, she decided to clean up the mess instead and picked up the junk closest to her.

"Wait!" Startled, she looked up at Jonas, who was at her side in a few steps. Sophie couldn't help flinching, but Jonas pretended not to notice. Instead, he put his hand on an armchair, straightening it up. "The least I can do is tidy up before I go. And I'll pay for the damage, of course. Don't worry about it."

"You haven't even been paid yet," Sophie retorted, and Jonas shrugged. "I don't see much broken. That vase was way ugly, anyway. You don't know how many times I've wanted to throw it away." She didn't want to comment on the fact that he was planning to move out again. In truth, she wouldn't mind if he did.

As he picked up the magazines he had swept off the table, he asked cautiously, "Throwing things away doesn't seem to be your thing?"

Sophie, who was in the process of picking her stuff off the floor and onto the re-erected armchair, looked up indignantly. "What do you mean by that?"

"Well, the shoes, for one thing." Embarrassed, Jonas shrugged and managed a pathetic smile. "You were quite relieved when I gave them back to you."

Sophie looked down at her shoes. They were so worn through that her toes were already showing. The pink paint had faded and been replaced by the dirt of the streets. To make matters worse, one of the straps had come loose and was hanging to the ground in an unsightly manner. "They were my mother's," she heard herself say.

"Oh. I see."

As he turned his back on her to straighten a side table, Sophie's eyes widened in shock. An ugly scar travelled over his right shoulder blade, bulging slightly as he tensed his muscles. The sight horrified her, and she found it hard to imagine the injury that had caused it.

"Sophie?" Confused, Sophie looked up and noticed Jonas was glancing over his shoulder. "Is everything alright?"

"Y-yes," she stammered, blood rushing to her cheeks. "I just... You were injured?"

Jonas tried to catch a glimpse of the scar himself. "Oh, that. Yeah, I got hit once. But..." He sighed again. "I was lucky and escaped with my life."

"Woah!" It slipped out of her mouth before Sophie could check herself. Annoyed, she clicked her tongue. Even if she didn't feel comfortable around Jonas, he deserved some sensitivity. "I mean, I'm sorry about that."

In response, Jonas just shrugged—his answer to everything. "Yeah, it's hard to see the good in it sometimes."

The enormity of his words almost took Sophie's breath away, and all at once, her passion was reignited. "Hey, you can't think like that!" She put her hands on her hips and challenged him. "You were in the war, and you *survived*. You helped people and..." Briefly, she interrupted herself as he grimaced in pain again. "You're alive. That's good. That's great!" she added vehemently.

Swallowing, Jonas struggled to find the next words. "You don't understand. I... Sophie, I wasn't a hero."

"So what?" she asked, shrugging. "Not everyone can be." She snorted. "Though honestly, in my opinion, everyone who risks their life for others is definitely a hero."

Jonas shook his head. "All I did was follow orders and hope I didn't get hit. That's not heroism."

"But you're alive," Sophie repeated, feeling chastened.

Gasping, Jonas took a breath. "This life?" His gaze travelled the room in hopelessness until it came to rest on her. "What am I doing with my life? I wander from place to place, job to job. I've started a degree and given up twice. I've had to leave four flats so far because my nightmares were too violent, and now I'm getting paid to tell your father you have a boyfriend."

Shock froze Sophie to the spot. All she could think of was a clumsy reply. "Can you please not tell him?" When Jonas looked at her dumbfounded, she added, "He doesn't have to know everything, does he? Besides, I'd like to tell him myself if I have to." She bit her lip, upset that he knew about Luca. Or had he just guessed what would drive her to The DeModie every night?

"Yes, of course." Awkwardly, Jonas rubbed the back of his neck. "I'm going to have to quit, anyway." When Sophie stared at him in confusion, he gestured briefly at the things she was picking up. "I can hardly stay here."

Hesitantly, Sophie straightened up again. Just a few minutes ago she had wanted nothing more than for him to leave. Now it seemed wrong. Jonas needed the job and a flat he could stay in. A place where he could feel safe one day. After all, she wasn't going to be here during the night, anyway.

"You don't have to go, you know." Sophie tried to look decisively nonchalant. "You said yourself that you don't normally have fits like that. This was an exception, wasn't it?"

Jonas nodded. "Yes, definitely." Then he screwed up his face and replied honestly, "I won't lie. Apparently, I sometimes scream in my sleep and lash out in bed, but I don't usually trash rooms." He turned away in shame before quietly admitting, "You're more likely to find me cowering in a corner because I'm afraid the ceiling will fall on my head."

Sophie smiled pityingly. His concession took away some of her terror. "You're safe here, Jonas. As far as I'm concerned, you can stay as long as you like. Until you're better and regardless of whether my father hired you." She rolled her eyes. "I will talk to him, though. Not about you, but the fact that he hires people to suss out my private life. That shouldn't be one of your duties." A crazy thought occurred to her. Frowning, Sophie looked at Jonas. "There's more to this job, right?"

To her relief, he hurried to say, "Yes, the contract says I'm supposed to take care of merchandise deliveries, and all the odds and ends that go on in the office. This was just supposed to be some sort of entry level test. I think he's pretty desperate."

"He's a bloody helicopter father who can't stand not knowing my every move," Sophie returned bitingly. Taking a deep breath, she struggled to explain a little more calmly. "I'm sorry. He just exaggerates so much. That's why I moved out." She sighed. "Tell him about The DeModie for all I care, so he can be at peace. But leave out the thing about Luca! Please!" she added, a little belatedly. She didn't want to imagine what would become of the curse if her father decided to forbid her to dance with Luca.

"Are you sure you want me around?" asked Jonas.

"I would say otherwise if I didn't, wouldn't I?"

For a moment, Sophie feared he would fall into her arms in sheer gratitude. But Jonas pulled himself together and kept it at a nod. "Thank you. That's quite generous of you. I promise I only need a few weeks, or maybe a month or two. So, he'll give me the recommendation." Jonas sighed heavily. "I'm pathetic, aren't I?"

"No," Sophie replied, smiling. "You're only trying to get back on your feet." A yawn came over her all at once as the last bit of tension fell away from her. "Well, I should get to bed, or I'll be asleep all day. Besides, I need to be fit for tonight."

"You're going dancing again?" Jonas asked in surprise.

Sophie tensed slightly. "Why not? As you said, I have a boyfriend and we... like to go dancing. I like dancing." She wasn't going to tell him about Luca's curse. He would probably think she was gullible or stupid.

"You dance beautifully," Jonas said instead, a pensive expression in his eyes.

The unexpected compliment brought a blush to her face. "Oh, nonsense. I'm completely out of practice."

Jonas smirked a little. "You sure about that? It looked to me like you were a professional."

The observation hit her as surprisingly as his compliment. It had been years since she had followed that dream. "I don't." That dream had died with her mother. "I only dance for myself and Luca." The smile returned to her lips at the thought of her prince. "Mostly for Luca."

Jonas turned his attention back to the mess. "I see. He's the one, I guess."

Sophie snorted. "No, he's just a true... I mean, he treats me like a princess." Jonas' sceptical look said a lot, and once again, the blood rushed to Sophie's cheeks. "Yeah, I know: pink tutu, ballet, daddy's little princess, now a prince. I'm a total cliché."

He tried to hide it, but Sophie could see the amusement in his eyes, and the longer they looked at each other, the more his mouth twisted into a grin.

"Go ahead and make fun of me," Sophie complained, but she couldn't really be angry with him. She was so relieved to see him smiling after all that darkness. The gleam in his eyes remained, and Sophie clicked her tongue. "All I meant was that Luca is really kind. He's a true gentleman, even pays the bill for me, and yes, he can dance." The smile in Jonas' eyes was disappearing. The mood threatened to tip again. "Anyway, he makes me feel very comfortable."

"That's great," Jonas said, with a seriousness that reminded her more of a funeral service than congratulations. "You can bring him home, by the way. I mean, it's your place, but I don't mind. You don't have to hide him because of me."

"We like to dance," Sophie hastily pushed as an excuse. "Really. We're happiest on the dance floor."

Judging by his expression, Jonas didn't believe a word she said. He tilted his head sceptically. "Are you afraid I'll tell your father? I promised not to tell him about Luca, didn't I? And if you want to bring a man home, that's your business?"

Sophie hesitated. No one could meet Luca. At least not for the next nine months. "We're not there yet." In her mind, she scolded herself for the excuse. As if their relationship was any of this stranger's business.

Jonas knitted his eyebrows and nodded slightly. "Well, then. You were going to bed, weren't you? I'll clean up the rest."

His sudden withdrawal puzzled Sophie, but she was too tired to dwell on it. "Okay. I'll see you later, then."

"See you later, Sophie," Jonas replied with a thin smile that didn't quite reach his eyes.

As she walked into her room and closed the door, she thought about what she had experienced. The past few hours had been overwhelming. First Luca's confession and then the confrontation with Jonas' war trauma. She wasn't sure which of the two she pitied more, but at least Luca didn't ask so many awkward questions.

Sophie dropped onto the bed and took off her broken shoes. For a long time, she hadn't thought about the day she had last stood on a stage. Back when she had worn her own shoes and not her mother's broken ones. With a sigh, she hung the shoes on the nail in the wall and began to get ready for bed.

With his compliment, Jonas had opened a wound that she'd thought had healed a long time ago. Dancing with Luca had always been such a dreamlike experience that she'd never noticed how much she missed the elegant shapes of ballet, the discipline of hours of practice, or the excitement before a performance.

Slipping into bed, Sophie took her mother's picture from the bedside table. It had been taken at a performance. Immersed in the music, her mother's face was deep in concentration, her body a work of art of curved lines. The notes of unheard music sounded in Sophie's mind, and in her imagination she flew back to the stage. There, under the spotlights, surrounded by the audience, she had known every step and turn. Now, the only way she knew was the one that led her into Luca's arms.

"Good night, Mum," Sophie whispered. Even before she had fallen asleep, the melody of The DeModie had replaced the one in her mind.

Chassé

"Every night, sir." Jonas stood to attention in front of Sophie's father two weeks later and reported to him. The delay had been necessary to avoid awkward questions around the fact that he'd known where she went each night straightaway. As he had promised Sophie, he had kept quiet about Luca. After all, that was none of his or her father's business.

Mr Kallenbach sat behind his desk, his eyes fixed on his computer screen. "What did you say the name of this club was?"

"The DeModie. It's on Niemeyer Street," Jonas answered promptly, then waited for Mr Kallenbach to type the address into the computer.

It didn't surprise Jonas when Mr Kallenbach said almost accusingly, "There is no club named The DeModie on Niemeyer Street or anywhere else."

"I'm not surprised. The club is very exclusive, bordering on the extreme, and quite particular about its visitors," Jonas explained, withholding the information that he had managed to get in. "They might be deliberately suppressing their address."

"Hmm, perhaps they're listed under a different name." Sophie's father sat back and regarded Jonas, his hands clasped under his chin. "What do you think of my daughter?"

The question hit Jonas out of left field. His mouth dropped open as he struggled to find the words. "I... Well," he stammered. Involuntarily, memories of Sophie pirouetting came to him. Her merry laughter rang in his ears. "Well..."

Mr Kallenbach rolled his eyes, disgruntled. "I asked for your opinion. Be honest and stop stuttering like a schoolboy!"

Jonas' ears burned with shame. "I-I..." He pulled himself together. "She seems to be a very cheerful person. Quite light-hearted."

"Her mother died two years ago," her father replied dryly.

Jonas stared at him, speechless. He had known that the shoes Sophie wore every day were her mother's, but not that she had died. Nevertheless, he stuck to his assessment. Unlike himself, Sophie was a fountain of life. Always happy, always exhilarated. "She seems to have dealt with it quite well."

Mr Kallenbach snorted. "Then why did she drop out of ballet school?" So, she had danced professionally, after all. "Not that I care much about that school. I'd be happy if she'd decided to do something sensible instead. But here we are, and she does absolutely nothing except spend my money in dance clubs night after night."

Jonas knew he had no business questioning Mr Kallenbach's parenting, but the way he spoke about the life choices of his grown-up daughter urged him to come to her defence. "She might need some time to figure out what she wants to do with her life."

"At my expense?" asked Mr Kallenbach.

Jonas was about to ask him why he didn't just cut her off then, but he held his tongue and bit down on the words. He was here to work, not interfere in family affairs.

Her father regarded Jonas thoughtfully. "What did you say she was? Light-hearted, right?"

Jonas nodded.

"I wish she was a little weighted down. She's aimless and addicted to dancing." Mr Kallenbach shook his head. "It ruins people."

"Excuse me?" Jonas dared to inquire, but Mr Kallenbach waved him off.

Instead, he leaned forward. "You're doing a good job, Jonas. You found out where my daughter always disappears to. Listen. I want you to keep me informed of her every move from now on."

Horrified, Jonas shook his head. He needed the job and more so the recommendation, but this was going too far. In his mind, he slammed his hands on the desk and lectured Mr Kallenbach on privacy. Instead, he gritted his teeth until he was sure he had his emotions under control and he could reply in a calm manner, "I won't spy on your daughter. Not for all the money in the world. If I might make a suggestion; why don't you talk to her?"

Mr Kallenbach rolled his eyes again and sank back into his office chair. "You seem very sure of yourself."

But he wasn't. In fact, Jonas felt sick at the prospect of what would happen now. He would be fired and have to look for a new job again. Just when he felt he had arrived for the first time in a long while. The thought of never hearing Sophie's laughter again turned his stomach into knots.

Mr Kallenbach snorted again. "Fine by me. I'll see you here Monday morning at eight sharp."

Jonas couldn't believe his luck. Hesitantly, he took a step back. "See you Monday, then."

Mr Kallenbach merely nodded and had already diverted his attention elsewhere. Jonas noticed that his gaze was resting on a picture frame on the desk. All at once, the office seemed too small for the two of them. Jonas was about to open the door when Mr Kallenbach looked up once more. "Jonas."

"Yes?" His heart was in his throat again.

"Take care of her, will you? She doesn't seem to be pushing you away."

Jonas hesitated, but then pulled himself together and stood to attention. "Of course. You can count on me."

The conversation with Sophie's father was still running through his mind as Jonas watched Sophie twirl around the small ballet studio after lunch. He was sitting against the wall, a drawing pad on his knees that had been lying forgotten on the bottom of his travel bag for years. Now, with a pencil in his hand, he sketched the jumps and pirouettes Sophie was performing. He was attempting to capture the magical moment when her movements aligned perfectly with the music. On their own, both music and dancer were impressive, but in combination, they sent a pleasant shiver down Jonas' spine.

It was Sophie's joy when she danced and the way she seemed completely absorbed in the music that inspired him. The passion with which she pursued dancing fascinated him as much as her vehement assertion that ballet meant no more to her than any other form of dance. When she danced with Luca, she wasn't doing ballet. Nevertheless, that was the style Jonas admired most. In ballet, it was only Sophie and the music.

After the rocky start, they had become used to each other and Jonas' nightmares had returned to a normal level. Sophie was opening up more, making him feel as if they'd been friends forever, even though she wasn't always truthful about her desire to dance or more personal matters. Instead, she constantly raved about Luca. By now, Jonas was convinced that Luca was one of those rich snobs who preyed on girls in dark clubs, paying for their drinks just to get into their pants. But for Sophie, he was the love of her life.

Jonas would have given a lot to be that naïve again, to be able to dive into any kind of passion. Unlike Sophie, he felt terribly empty, and if he looked too deep within, he found only darkness. He had no idea what would await him if Mr

Kallenbach ever had enough of him. Until then, he enjoyed the bright spot in his life that was Sophie.

"What are you drawing?" Her voice snapped Jonas out of his thoughts. Hastily, he flipped the pad back to his earlier sketches as she came towards him. There was a mischievousness glint in Sophie's eyes. She caught a glimpse of the drawing, only to be disappointed. "Houses?"

The sheet on top was an ancient sketch of a building. The central piece was a round tower that had a vaguely medieval look, but sat in an elongated building that gave it a more modern edge. A small notation of the date in the corner told him the sketch had been drawn in his last year at school.

Before Jonas could stop her, Sophie had grabbed the pad and leaned against the wall next to him to flick through the sketches; fortunately for him, in the wrong direction. He wasn't ready to explain why he'd drawn her if she discovered the pictures of herself. Instead, more building sketches followed, some technical, some almost artistic, depending on what his mind had come up with at the time. "Where's that?"

He had no choice but to stand up and check the pad in her hand. "This?" The fruity, pungent aroma of Sophie's shampoo hit his nose, and Jonas struggled to concentrate on the sketch of a gallery supported by columns. "Nowhere."

"Nowhere?" Sophie inquired, amused.

"Well, no one's built it yet," he replied modestly, then added, "and I'm sure no one ever will. These are just sketches."

She turned to him and returned the sketch pad before she got to the discriminating pictures of her. "So, did you want to become an architect?"

Jonas took the drawings, trying his best not to touch Sophie's fingers as he did so. "Not really, no. Although," he remembered, "when I was ten or so, I did want to be an architect for a while. It sounded cool."

"Then why didn't you become one?" Sophie asked with interest.

With a shrug, Jonas said, "Well, architecture was just a pipe dream, a childhood fantasy. Pretty much my entire family was in the army. My father and my big brother still are. For as long as I can remember, they told me how important military service is and how too few people signed up for it. There was never any question of me doing anything else." And now he wished he had done anything but that.

Jonas didn't want to see the pitying look that followed. Pity was for the victims the war had claimed, or the orphans in Afghanistan. Not for cowards like him.

"I see," Sophie murmured hesitantly. "What do they say about you being here now?"

And just like that, she had hit his sore spot. "No one's ever asked me that." He rubbed his hand over his chin. "They don't have a clue. They probably still think I'm doing my Economics degree."

His answer was met with confusion. "Why?"

Because he was a coward who couldn't face the disappointment. Jonas stared at the ground, searching for the right words.

"It's complicated. I... I feel like I've come home from the war as someone else. Like I'm no longer the Jonas they knew."

"Because of the nightmares?"

Jonas swallowed hard. "That, too." The memories of the few meetings with his family since his return from Afghanistan left a strangely bitter taste on his tongue. "My father is disappointed that I was discharged, even if he doesn't say so. It's difficult to explain. Somehow we suddenly have nothing to talk about." He'd felt like a stranger even in his own room.

"Parents are difficult in general," Sophie agreed, making Jonas laugh. "Hey, I have an idea. Let's enjoy the nice weather and go outside."

"Go outside?" he asked, puzzled. His gaze drifted to the window. Out there, the trees were clad in reds, oranges, and yellows.

Sophie nodded enthusiastically. "Yes, let's go for a walk. You and me, a bit of chatting and fresh air. Do you want to come?"

"Sure, I do."

~

Although the trees were already wearing their autumn coat, the sun was pleasantly warm, making jackets almost superfluous. Sophie walked beside him, her hands in her pockets. From time to time, she kicked a pine cone in front of her. Every now and then, Jonas stole a glance at her face and found her smiling blissfully, enjoying the sun's rays. At the sight, his throat tightened in a way he hadn't experienced in a long time, and he hastily turned his attention back to the forest path in front of them.

"Did you get shot?" Sophie asked out of the blue, studying his reaction with interest.

It took Jonas a while to sort his thoughts enough to know what she was talking about. "Not directly. It was an explosion in a house. I was outside in the street and got hit by shards of glass. The whole thing was pretty bad." The words rolled off his tongue surprisingly easily. It was more difficult to hold back the images that followed. The building involved had been a makeshift clinic, and the horrific screams still echoed in his head.

Sophie regarded him thoughtfully before shaking her head. "It's so hard to imagine what you've been through. Almost as if it happened in another world. Crazy." Fascinated, she shook her head.

"Unfortunately, it's ours." The cynicism tasted bitter on his tongue. Jonas hardly recognised himself.

"As I said, really hard to imagine." Unlike him, Sophie sounded casual. The memories had no power over her, and his tales were nothing more than horror stories.

Suddenly Sophie smiled at him. "I'm glad you made it back alive."

Her honest statement warmed Jonas' heart, and he couldn't help but smile. He had doubted the truth of those words far too often. That Sophie voiced them made them easier to believe. "Thank you."

For reasons he couldn't fathom, Sophie shook her head and smirked, before she unceremoniously linked arms with him. "You should remind yourself of that. You're alive. The war is behind you."

An answer stuck in his throat as, all of a sudden, it turned dry. Blood rushed into Jonas' ears as he searched for the fleeting words. He was too aware of the arm at his side. "When you say it like that it sounds so simple," he finally managed to say.

"The key is to look forward and stop looking back," was Sophie's prompt reply. Already she seemed to give no more thought to his gruesome memories.

Chuckling, Jonas rubbed the back of his neck with his free hand. "How do you do that?"

"Do what, exactly?"

"Not overthink anything. You just leave everything behind and never look back," Jonas explained, still with a smile on his lips.

Sophie furrowed her brow. "I'm going to pretend that was a compliment." Before Jonas could justify himself, she laughed and poked his side. "Would do you some good, if you ask me." Then she shrugged. "I *do* think. Just not all the time and about everything. I like to be spontaneous and enjoy life." With a perky glint in her eye, she added, "Drinking helps, too."

Jonas snorted, unable to take her seriously any longer.

"No, really," Sophie stressed. "You need to loosen up a bit. Or dance. It always helps me to dance it all out."

"I don't dance," Jonas replied firmly.

Sophie sighed heavily and rolled her eyes. "It doesn't hurt anyone to dance."

Her exaggerated facial expression made him laugh again. "I'm really bad at it. And looking at how damn well you dance makes me want to make an ass of myself even less."

Again, Sophie shook her head and chuckled.

"By the way," he remembered. "Your father said you went to ballet school. I mean, it was obvious that you didn't learn to dance like that on your own."

Gasping, Sophie's eyes snapped open. "I most certainly did not! There are many, many years of disciplined training behind it. Five, heck, seven times a week, always the same steps." She shuddered, as if the very thought made her uncomfortable. "You get so fed up with it, eventually."

It did sound quite exhausting, and yet, Jonas didn't believe that she hated it. Why else would she still be exercising almost daily in her little studio? "So, you're glad that's behind you?"

"Oh yes! School was terrible. You were never allowed to have fun or be young. I mean, we weren't even allowed to go out on weekends because, apparently, they could see it on Monday." She grimaced exaggeratedly.

Jonas laughed. "Sounds really horrible. Good riddance."

Sophie playfully swatted at him. Chuckling, Jonas dodged her hand and disengaged his arm. Putting her hands on her hips, she huffed indignantly at him as he walked backwards in front of her, just out of reach. "You think this is funny? Teasing me like that?" she exclaimed.

He couldn't help but snort. "Teasing you? Because I don't believe you when you say it was all so terrible?"

"It was awful!" Sophie asserted vigorously, before finally relenting. "Fine, it wasn't all horrible. Performing was fun, but all the training before that... No thanks!"

"Mmm," was all Jonas said as the corners of his mouth inevitably pulled upwards.

"Jonas!" The very next moment she had bent down and thrown a pine cone at him.

Surprised, Jonas ducked.

Sophie already had the next load in her hand, grinning. "I'll get you with the next one."

Amused, Jonas shook his head. "No, you won't." Laughing, he took cover as her retort came in the form of pine cones, then gathered ammunition to return the shots.

⚬

"We could watch a movie. I don't have to leave for another three hours," Sophie said when they had returned home. There were still some fir needles and leaves in her hair, and her cheeks were flushed. In Jonas' eyes, there was no image more beautiful, and his fingers itched to capture it on paper.

He took off his jacket and slid his shoes next to the door. "Sounds good. I'll cook us something and you pick one."

"Oooh, I'm getting a homemade meal," Sophie commented, wriggling her eyebrows.

"Sure, but don't get used to it," Jonas grumbled playfully and made his way to the kitchen, while Sophie ran her fingers through her hair to get rid of the leaves and then looked through her film collection.

A little later, when he had just put the water on, she held up a film. Sceptically, Jonas asked, "A dance film? Do we have to?"

"Yes. Besides, you're gonna love it. You watch me dancing almost every day," Sophie answered cheekily and went over to the TV.

Jonas blushed with embarrassment and quickly bent down to check on the cans. His growing feelings for Sophie were going to get him into hot water. As soon as the music drifted through the apartment, he was magically drawn to the small ballroom and could think of nothing better than watching Sophie dance. But that didn't mean he enjoyed watching dance films.

The film wasn't quite as bad as he had expected, even if he would've preferred something else. Sophie, on the other hand, followed every movement on the screen with shining eyes. Watching her captivated Jonas much more than the half-baked drama. He contemplated putting his arm around her and pulling her close to him. But then he remembered Luca and how much Sophie adored him.

"Did you do something like that?" he asked after a quick glance at the TV, where the two main characters were dancing together in the street, performing impressive acrobatics.

"Hush." Spellbound, Sophie stared at the screen. Her eyes reflected their movements, and Jonas held his breath.

Suddenly, shots rang through the air, and the world disappeared. Hot dust burned in his lungs as he threw himself to the ground and took cover behind a remnant of wall. Grenades flew over their heads and Jonas folded his arms above his head in despair. His breath came in short bursts. His gaze flitted back and forth.

A bomb hit the building behind him and splinters rained down on him. There were screams, strangely distorted in the thick dust around him. People ran around, threw themselves on the ground and never got up again. A command went unheard when the next explosion hit close to him. The heat hit him in the face and blinded him.

Then someone grabbed him and shook him. "Jonas!"

Jonas looked up and caught sight of his comrade. Blood was dripping down Philipp's face from under his helmet. In his eyes, he saw the same horror that was burning through his stomach. "Jonas!" the long-dead friend called again.

Sudden pain stung his cheek. Jonas turned his head back and now saw his friend's features slowly blurring, becoming softer and more feminine. Sophie.

He pulled her close and held her tight until her heartbeat was all he could hear. The life in her drove away the images of death and destruction like a mother's hand drives away the ghosts of the night. The fruity scent of her hair replaced the metallic smell of blood and slowly, the dust cleared.

Jonas found himself lying on the floor between the couch and coffee table in Sophie's living room. The silly movie was still playing on the TV, the couple arguing in the hospital. Slowly, Jonas realised that the shots had been part of the story.

"Are you all right?" Sophie asked, her breath hot and alive against his neck.

He still held her close in a desperate attempt to fill the void left in him by the deaths he had witnessed. Try as he might, he was unable to let go. He needed her, needed her more than he had ever needed anyone. Just to know he was still alive.

"Jonas?" Her voice sounded very timid.

It took him an enormous effort to release his tense jaw muscles and remember that his teeth had no reason to chatter. "Yes?"

Relieved, Sophie sighed and turned her head so that her forehead came to rest on his shoulder. He didn't give her much more room to move. "You scared me."

Jonas didn't know how to answer her. He could barely open his mouth.

Again, they were silent as the movie played forgotten in the background. Slowly, the tension eased, and his thoughts returned to reality. The weight on his chest was Sophie, not a piece of debris. Hesitantly, he began to loosen his grip.

"Jonas?" she asked again, and he managed to turn his head so he could look at her. There was a sudden sadness in her eyes. "You were right. I do miss it."

Confused, he frowned. "What do you mean?"

"The stage," she breathed. "The music, all the training. I *do* miss it. But only a little. Very little."

Pas de trois

Her feet ached, and yet, Sophie wouldn't have left her prince's arms for anything in the world. Together, they spun and swayed through the melody, their gaze firmly locked. Like a puppeteer, The DeModie's music led them through the dance. Sophie never missed a step, her posture never slackened, and the blissful smile on her lips never faded.

But The DeModie had changed. The fairy tale-like gold and silver forest still watched over the entrance and dancers still floated over the enchanted mirror lake in front of the romantic castle. But there were fewer dancers than before. The light was dim. Instead, other figures crowded the lakeside and followed her movements with blank stares. Sophie shuddered in the face of their longing.

"Winter," Luca spoke in his velvety voice and immediately her attention returned to him. "Fewer people come to The DeModie. Their light is missed in the darkness."

"That doesn't sound so good," Sophie commented. He pulled her close, and she placed her hands on his chest.

Luca smiled, and the doubt she had felt a moment ago was a memory in the wind. "It is what it is. The dark season. I usually can't stand it, but this time I have you. And you're all the light I need."

Smirking, Sophie rolled her eyes. "Old charmer," she scolded, and Luca grinned. But then he leaned down, and all at once, Sophie's heart beat faster. She lost herself in the dreamy blue of his eyes and then she felt his lips on hers.

Someone grabbed her by the arm and pulled Sophie out of her bliss.

"Where is she?" she was asked in a gruff voice as fingers dug painfully into her arm. Startled, Sophie recognised Frederick, one of the other princes trapped in The DeModie. So far, they had barely spoken to each other, but Sophie knew he was a wee bit older than Luca.

"Ow, you're hurting me!"

Frederick's piercing look, however, made her swallow heavily. With stoic calm, Luca stepped between them and loosened Frederick's grip.

The latter sullenly repeated his question. "Where is she?" The urgency in his voice startled Sophie. "Your friend. Paula... Pia." The fact that he didn't know her name offhand made Sophie uncomfortable. Pia and he had danced with each other every night for many months.

Sophie shook her head slightly and saw panic flash in his eyes. "She doesn't like it here anymore. Her feet hurt, and she has exams coming up. She needs all her energy for classes."

It wasn't fair of Pia to leave him hanging like that, without even an explanation, but then again, she didn't know about the curse. Frederick had eventually tired her with his desire to see her every night, and the mesmerising spell of The DeModie had worn off. Supposedly, Pia had tried to compromise at first, by suggesting some variety in the choice of their nightly hangouts. But of course, that had fallen on deaf ears, and today Sophie's friends had decided to go somewhere else. Sophie was just as unenthusiastic about it as Frederick, feeling similarly abandoned. Yet she'd known it was only a matter of time before they dropped her. Too many things separated them since she'd stopped going to ballet school.

"She's not coming anymore?" For a moment, Frederick was too shocked for more words.

Luca gave him a sombre look and pulled Sophie back onto the dance floor. The music settled in her muscles, and although her thoughts were still with Frederick, her body was yearning to move.

"Never again?" At the desperation in Frederick's voice, Sophie's stomach turned.

"I'm sorry," she whispered, placing a hand on the back of Luca's neck. Frederick's reaction to Pia's abandonment only strengthened Sophie's resolve to never do the same to Luca. For him, she would continue dancing, even if her feet bled.

Once again, Frederick tore her from her warm embrace, and this time, Luca lost his grip on her hand. The rhythm pounded in her stomach as Frederick took the lead, swinging her around and throwing her high into the air. Several times, she tried to break free, but he always pulled her back with an iron grip.

"What do you think you're doing, Frederick?" Luca shouted, the anger in his voice making Sophie tremble.

She didn't understand what was happening to her, but after the next twirl, it was Luca who caught her and spun her around to rhythms that made her pulse beat faster.

Another change in the music brought her back into Frederick's arms. "She's dancing with me now, Luca. You can wait, but I can't take it anymore."

The blood in Sophie's veins throbbed in time with the strings and winds of a classical ballet, driving her faster and more wildly into higher lifts and leaps in Frederick's arms.

Then Luca's arms encircled her again and calm returned. "Sophie is my partner."

Panting, Sophie pressed herself against Luca's chest. Sweat trickled down her back and conflicting melodies droned in her head.

"Please. It's my only chance if I don't want to start over. I can't do it anymore." Frederick's hand closed around Sophie's wrist, and with a jerk, her body arched in his direction against her will.

Luca immediately pulled her back, his eyes blazing with righteous anger. For one insane moment, Sophie wished she could split in two under the tension and make both princes happy. Not even the music could decide which of the two it preferred.

"No!" Both brothers froze as the word passed her lips like the beat of a drum. Panting, Sophie propped herself up on her knees. Finally, she took a deep breath and looked up at Frederick. "I'm dancing this year with Luca and no one else."

As if she had struck him fatally, Frederick sank to the floor.

Suddenly, Tomas and one of the other brothers were there and grabbed Frederick's shoulders. He looked up at her in desperation, but Sophie did nothing as the brothers dragged him off the dance floor. He threw himself against their grip, even then arching expressively, showing what a talented dancer he was with every movement of his body, and yet he couldn't stop them from taking him to the castle, which looked nothing like a backdrop now. The dark battlements towered menacingly, and the sight of them made Sophie's blood run cold.

She trembled as she watched Frederick disappear into the castle, screaming and flailing. Luca stepped in front of her and blocked her view. Her legs gave way, and in the next moment, she was clinging to him. Suddenly, she was terrified of losing him to the castle, too.

Luca managed to calm her pulse, which had been raised dramatically by her dancing. He stroked her hair and swayed with her across the dance floor. Further and further away from the dark castle, he led her towards the enchanting gold and silver trees whose leaves tinkled with music.

Slowly, her heart rate slowed and her breathing was no longer ragged. Her mind was with Luca, and the music was a gentle, dream-like melody, ideal for the romantic dance of two lovers.

"I'm sorry you had to see that," Luca whispered in her ear.

Sophie wrapped her arms around him to be closer to him. "What's going to happen to him now?" Even though he had been rough with her, she felt sorry for Frederick.

"They'll calm him down first. Comfort him. Then he has to hope another girl will stray here and that she'll finally be the one to set him free." Luca's voice was full of compassion, and Sophie detected a few sad notes in the melody.

As if of their own accord, her feet slipped into the turns Luca was gently leading her into. "I hope he finds the right one someday."

"I hope so, too, but he doesn't have many more opportunities." When Sophie looked at him puzzled, he continued, "He's been stood up too many times. His hopes have been dashed so often... I don't know if he has the strength left to dance for a whole year." He guided Sophie through his raised arm. "You've experienced first-hand how much he longs for the daylight."

Luca's hands were on the small of her back, holding her effortlessly as she arched her back. "And you? Have you been disappointed too?" asked Sophie curiously.

For a moment, a shadow flitted across his face before he pulled her close again and pressed her against his chest. Very quietly, he answered, "Only once. After two months, she lost interest. I never saw her again."

"Just like that?" asked Sophie, putting her arms around him.

"It's always like that. They come for a few weeks, then they move on. Hardly any of them have the will to dance for a year," Luca explained with a touch of bitterness.

It was more than Sophie could bear. Hastily, she promised, "I'll do it. I won't let you down, Luca. Never." She looked deep into his eyes, hoping he'd see the truth in her words. "Summer or winter; I'll dance with you until the curse is broken and I can take you outside with me. And then we'll keep dancing until the end of our days."

The smile that blossomed on his face was like a balm to her soul. "Will you tell me what it's like outside? I miss the sunlight painting the world in colour."

"Well, in that case, I'm afraid I'll have to disappoint you," she began to report. "Right now, the world is all grey. It rains most of the day, and I'm convinced the sun will hide behind the clouds until spring."

"Rain?" asked Luca, a gleam in his eyes.

Sophie giggled, back to her usual self. "You know, water falling from the sky?"

Luca shook his head. "I forgot about it a long time ago. It sounds wonderful. Magical."

"Ew, no. It's cold and wet and uncomfortable. I'd much rather be in your arms than out there in the rain." To back up her words, she snuggled closer to him. "But soon, the snow will come, and it will dress the world in white, rivalling the beauty in here. At least when it's freshly fallen." It had snowed when she'd lain her mother to rest.

"I'd like to see that," Luca whispered with unbearable longing, and Sophie was convinced she would never let him down.

When Sophie left The DeModie the next morning, her head was dizzy from the events of the previous night. The music still reverberated in her ears, strangely distorted by the influence of alcohol. It was as if The DeModie didn't want to let her go.

Again and again, Sophie looked over her shoulder, unable to shake the feeling she was being followed. But there was no one in the shadows and not a soul on the streets.

Luca had said that nothing could leave The DeModie. Nevertheless, Sophie quickened her steps, looking back more often than forward, when suddenly she bumped into an unexpected obstacle and cried out in surprise. Hands grabbed her, stopping her from stumbling backwards. In a wild panic, Sophie began to kick out and hit her attacker with her handbag.

"What the... Sophie!" the man hissed in pain.

Startled, Sophie paused. This wasn't a shadow that had followed her out of The DeModie. It was Jonas. She looked at him in confusion. "What are you doing here?"

Jonas let go of her now that she had calmed down and rubbed his cheekbone with a groan. "What do you have in there? Rocks?" When Sophie didn't answer and crossed her arms in front of her chest instead, he finally replied, "The sun has been up for a long time, and you weren't home. I got worried. Is everything all right?"

Sophie thought of the apprehensive feeling she had just experienced and swallowed. Meanwhile, the cold from the wet ground penetrated the thin soles of her shoes, pricking her feet like a thousand needles. "Yeah, sure. I just thought I saw something."

Concerned, Jonas peered in the direction she had come from, but didn't seem to spot anything. His gaze fell on her again. "Goodness, aren't you cold?"

"Yes, very," Sophie answered miserably, unable to stop her teeth from chattering. Apart from the fact that her pointe shoes were squishing more with each passing minute, she wore no tights under her short skirt and her thin jacket was barely adequate for the cold November weather. Last night, it hadn't been this cold.

Jonas made a sudden effort to lift her into his arms. "You'll never get home like this. Your shoes are soaked."

"Hey! What do you think you're doing?" Horrified, she batted his arms away.

Jonas shrugged sheepishly. "It's raining and you're cold. You'll get sick if you continue running around with wet feet."

Her feet were blocks of ice already. "Alright. But if I'm too heavy for you, you'll stop playing hero."

Jonas grinned and lifted her up in his arms.

Surprisingly, Sophie found it quite comfortable to let him carry her. Slowly, his warmth crept under her skin. Only her feet remained cold.

Sophie thought back to The DeModie. The hidden entrance suddenly seemed terribly threatening to her. "The underworld."

"Hmm?" asked Jonas, and Sophie became abruptly aware that she had spoken her thoughts aloud.

For a moment she hesitated, but the words wanted out of her. She had already been unable to tell her friends the truth. "The DeModie isn't a normal club." Bit by bit, Sophie began to tell him about the curse that had befallen its inhabitants and what had happened between Frederick and Luca.

Jonas listened stoically, never questioning, and endured her fantastic tale without batting an eyelid. Only when they were almost home did he finally give his opinion. "Sounds to me like Luca is pulling a lot of wool over your eyes. You got to admit that this curse is awfully convenient." When Sophie looked at him in confusion, he added, "That way you'll always have a reason to go back to him."

Sophie searched for jealousy in his eyes, but found none. All she could hear was concern. Unbearable concern that almost crushed her. Jonas' worried glance only made it worse. His arms suddenly seemed constricting.

Her increasing restlessness didn't go unnoticed by him, and he set her back down on the floor. "Sorry," he murmured. "I overstepped."

Sophie inhaled with a hiss as the cold shot back up her feet. "Shit, it's cold!"

The worry in Jonas' eyes only intensified. Hastily, Sophie turned away and hurried home. Jonas followed her a little more slowly, as if he didn't dare get too close.

Soon, Sophie's guilty conscience began to stir. Somewhat erratically, she took up the conversation again. "Luca wouldn't lie to me, and if you'd seen Frederick, there'd be no doubt in your mind either."

"If you say so," was all Jonas replied with, not doing her the favour of agreeing.

They arrived home, and he unlocked the door. Luca would have held it open for her, but Jonas entered first, switched on the light, and immediately went in search of a towel. Sophie followed him and sighed in relief as her toes sank into the warm carpet.

"So, does that mean you're going to dance there for another seven months?" Jonas asked as he returned, knelt down in front of her, and to her surprise, began rubbing her feet dry.

Sophie almost caught her breath. "Yes, until the end of May. That's when I met him this year."

"Mm." Again, there was little enthusiasm. "So, that's how long you'll continue to put yourself in danger?"

"Danger?" With a few exceptions, she hadn't found The DeModie particularly threatening.

Jonas looked up at her, the oppressive worry in his gaze again. "Well, you just said The DeModie was the underworld with demons and ghosts and stuff. You feel watched, maybe even hunted." He had taken her fanciful description in a stride.

With a shudder, Sophie remembered the hungry looks the other residents gave her far too often lately. She'd only managed to ignore them by snuggling close to her prince.

"I could bring you and pick you up if you like."

"What?" Hastily, she took a step back.

Jonas straightened up with a sigh. "Just in case a demon ambushes you outside. Luca can look after you inside. I get that, but he can't go outside, and it's cold and dark in winter." He mumbled something else, but she didn't quite catch it.

In fact, Sophie hoped she had misheard. "Excuse me?"

Jonas regarded her with his typical look of deep suffering. "I said you get drunk a lot."

Her nostrils quivered in anger. That was what she hated about other people's concerns. The accusations. The judgment. "Whether I'm drunk or not is none of your fucking business," she barked.

"But I promised your father I'd look after you," he explained.

Sophie was horrified. Suddenly, she couldn't breathe. Dangerously quiet, she repeated, "You what?"

"I have..." Embarrassed, Jonas rubbed the back of his neck. "It's not what you think. Your father merely asked me to look after you and I..." He seemed to realise he was making a mess out of this.

His calm voice alone drove Sophie up the wall. She didn't need a bodyguard. She certainly didn't need him.

"I'm going to take a shower," she announced, adding bitingly, "without an escort!"

⁓

The hot water had helped calm her mind and think about the things she'd been avoiding for too long. In the beginning, Jonas had been nothing more than a guy her father had forced on her. She liked him, even enjoyed living with him. What she didn't like was his occasional patronising attitude, hidden under a mask of concern.

Jonas had become an unexpected friend, and secretly she liked his quiet, thoughtful manner and the fact that he cared about her wellbeing, whether he was looking out for her for money or not. It had been a long time since Sophie had spoken this honestly to anyone about her ambitions and old dreams. She couldn't do it with her friends or Luca.

What did it mean to Luca, anyway, given the terrible curse he had to endure? It would be childish to mention her dreams when all he longed for was a day in the sun.

To Jonas, her dreams seemed to mean everything. He didn't stop asking about her dancing, watched her training almost every day, and soaked up her answers like a sponge. While his obsession with her life was a little disconcerting, she enjoyed the feeling of closeness it had created between them.

Somewhat mollified, she sat down at the breakfast table Jonas had set for her, as if she hadn't just thrown a hissy fit. "You know you don't have to do that, don't you?"

Jonas was sorting the fresh laundry, folding it neatly. Her flat never looked this tidy before he moved in. If she disregarded the mess he'd made on his first day.

"Yes, I do. Otherwise, I'd have to buy new things and throw away the dirty ones, and I don't have that kind of money."

She could see the hint of a grin on his face. "Very funny," Sophie said. Rolling her eyes in amusement, she corrected herself. "What I meant was the worrying about me. Carrying me home, looking after me."

Jonas paused for a moment. "I keep my promises."

"A promise." She could live with that. Maybe. "But you didn't sign a contract that stated you had to protect me 24/7 or some rubbish like that?" Who knew what her father might have come up with now?

Again, Jonas' dry sense of humour answered her: "Of course, I did. Paragraph 3.4: If Sophie ever gets caught in the rain, carry her home." He put down the washing and leaned against the back of the chair, smiling. "Any colds will be subtracted from my pay."

Giggling, Sophie almost choked on her roll. "Oh dear, there's no way I'll be fine with that." She raised both hands in a mock pledge. "I promise I'll put on a warmer jacket from now on…" Jonas raised his eyebrows. "And wear leggings."

"Sounds good." He smiled softly and turned back to his laundry. "I'd also suggest another pair of sturdier shoes, or I'll have to carry you again."

Sophie passed over the criticism of her shoes with a joke. "The way my feet hurt after dancing all night, I might take you up on that more often than you'd like."

Instead of laughing, Jonas frowned. "Do they hurt a lot?"

"A little. Well, it's kind of to be expected when you dance through every night, isn't it?" Sophie shrugged and finished her tea before stretching her arms, yawning. "I'd better go to sleep. I'm sure you have to leave for work soon."

"Yes, soon." He hesitated for a moment, then offered, "I can give you a massage if you like."

For a long time, Sophie looked at him, trying to discern his intentions. Jonas had always been so painfully honest that even now she could detect no false pretence. He only wanted to help her. An unfamiliar thought.

"Okay," she said, calling his bluff. Since the sofa was occupied by small piles of laundry, Sophie went to her room. "Are you coming?"

Jonas cleared his throat. Blushing, he put aside the T-shirt he was smoothing out. "I can't go into your room."

Grinning, Sophie said, "If it's to massage my feet, you can."

While she waited for him to follow her, Sophie crawled under the covers. She almost closed her eyes straight away. The days were getting shorter and shorter, leaving her hardly any time to sleep. She'd already had to give up training in the studio so she would be rested for the night. She was sure Luca wouldn't be thrilled if she fell asleep in his arms. She wondered what havoc that would mean for the curse.

When Jonas' weight lowered onto the mattress and he took her right foot in his hands, Sophie startled. She must have closed her eyes after all. With gentle but strong movements, he circled his thumb across the sole. Sophie sighed in relief. It felt good.

While Jonas silently massaged her feet, he gazed around the room until his gaze caught her mother's picture.

"That was fifteen years ago. She had the lead role in Sleeping Beauty," Sophie explained languidly.

Surprised, Jonas looked at her. "That's your mother? I thought it was you."

"Me?" she asked with amusement, suddenly much more alert. "What makes you think that? As if I've ever been the focus of photographers. I was still in training, after all."

"Well, aren't ballet dancers generally young?" he asked bluntly, changing to the other foot. "She reminds me of you. The way she raises her hands, the leg."

"Everyone looks like that. Any professional dancer should while they're holding that position," Sophie chided him gently.

Jonas shook his head. "Sorry, I didn't know that. She just looks like you when she does that."

Sophie regarded Jonas thoughtfully. Never before had she met someone that was so brutally honest and at the same time so hard on himself. His words had touched something in her, and the cosy warmth of the bed helped her open up a little. "I once wanted to be exactly like her. We argued a lot, but we were still very close."

"I never would have guessed, given how much you love her shoes," Jonas replied wryly. More gently, he asked, "How did she die?"

"MS," she replied with a sigh. Sensing his slight confusion, she elaborated, "Multiple sclerosis. First, it took away her dancing and then..." She tried to remember, but just thinking about it hurt. "Usually it's not fatal, not right away. But in rare cases it is, and my mother was one of those cases. All in all, it was quite quick."

"Quick is good," Jonas murmured softly. She knew he didn't mean her mother.

"It wasn't pretty, that's for sure. But it's the way it is." The words came easily to Sophie, rehearsed and spoken a hundred times.

As usual, Jonas saw right through her. "I'm sorry you lost her so soon."

Sophie waved it off. "It's been two years. Half a lifetime practically."

"Your father still worries about you." Gently, he covered her feet with the blanket.

"My father always worries about me," Sophie admitted. "Especially when it comes to dancing. He's afraid I'll get MS too and that dancing will break me like it broke her. But that's nonsense. One has nothing to do with the other, and MS isn't hereditary." Those were facts she knew well, and yet, she couldn't completely stave off the irrational fear. Her mother's pain had burned itself too deeply into her for that.

With some effort, Sophie tore her mind away from the unpleasant memories and buried them deep inside herself again. "You can massage my feet more often. That was wonderful."

Jonas laughed. "I'll keep it in mind." He stood up and looked down at her, smiling. "Good night, Sophie."

"Good day, Jonas," she replied. Later, she couldn't even remember that he had left the room.

Sur les pointes

The morning was still young when Jonas stretched his legs in front of The DeModie. Hands in his pockets, he waited impatiently for the sun to rise from the darkness. He stifled a yawn. How Sophie managed to dance through the increasingly long nights was a mystery to him. At least she had finally allowed him to pick her up, as the feeling of being watched whenever she left the club had only intensified. Although he now waited outside the club every morning just before dawn, Jonas had never seen the shadows Sophie spoke of.

With wet and cold weather abound, not many partygoers were to be seen this early. The people he saw were more likely to be on their way to work, if they passed through this street at all. The big nightclubs had closed hours ago, but the plain entrance between them was still busy. Jonas stood on the opposite side and looked at the strange figures that clustered around The

DeModie in the dark season. Unlike the other guests, they returned to the club at the end of the night instead of leaving.

There weren't many who braved the cold weather, but they all had something run down about them. Their hair and beards were matted, their clothes a grey-brown potpourri of patches, and in their hands, they often held a beer or cigarette. The shoes on their feet seemed as if they would fall apart just by looking at them. And almost all of them had stark bluish eyes that shone feverishly.

As the sky gradually lightened, Jonas made his way over. One by one, the figures disappeared into the darkness of The DeModie. Only the last of them, her eyes dark instead of blue, looked longingly at the grey sky until the door opened once more from the inside and the bouncer put his hand on her shoulder, comforting but firm.

His gaze crossed Jonas'. It was the same guy he'd met on his first visit. After the woman entered, the bouncer stood wide-legged and folded his arms. "You again."

"I'm not trying to enter," Jonas told him. The hostility with which the bouncer regarded him still confounded him, but he had no intention of taking the bait.

His counterpart snorted. "You think I don't see you hanging around here all the time? Leave our Sophie alone!"

"Your Sophie?" Jonas asked with a snort. "Does she belong to the whole club now? She's not going to dance with each of you for a year."

The bouncer's eyes narrowed, but before he could reply, the door opened again and Sophie came staggering out, laughing.

With a beaming smile, she turned to the bouncer. "See you tonight, Tomas!"

Tomas' face softened uncharacteristically as he smiled at Sophie. "See you tonight, Princess Sophie."

Sophie laughed in response. Jonas thought to himself how beautiful her laughter was that she could cheer not only him but also this curmudgeon.

"Jonas," she called out, her eyes shining as she spotted him. A little later, Sophie collapsed into his arms.

Her hot breath hit his face and the smell of alcohol filled his nostrils as she wrapped her arms around his neck. More by accident than intent, her lips brushed his, and for a moment, Jonas forgot everything else. The sweet taste of cocktails still clung to her mouth. Then Sophie buried her face against his shoulder again.

"Sophie."

She grinned at him, then swayed a little backward.

"You're drunk as a skunk." Like a beacon, reality spread through Jonas, burning away all thoughts of romance.

Laughing, Sophie stumbled back into his arms and Jonas just managed to catch her. A fleeting glance over her shoulder made his blood run cold. Tomas' blue eyes were burning through him. He had seen that look before; in the eyes of those who had lost everything in the war, including their humanity.

No longer caring about Sophie's drunken antics, Jonas carried her in his arms and strode down the street. His nerves were taut, as they always were when he entered enemy territory. The look of murder in Tomas's eyes was too vivid to shake.

The way Sophie had her arms wrapped around his neck and her breath moving across his skin distracted Jonas from his discomfort faster than he liked. "Hey, Sophie, save that for Luca!" he said hoarsely, and wanted to slap himself for it the next second.

Surprisingly, she understood what he meant and turned her head the other way. "Didn't mean to." The words hit like he'd been kicked in the stomach.

As Sophie clung to him in silence, Jonas' mind wandered back to the moment their lips had touched. The sweet taste still lingered on his lips, reminding him of what would never be. He would have given anything for her to have kissed him for real, not just drunkenly bump into him.

"Do you always have to get so drunk?" he whispered in frustration.

Her laughter rang through the early morning as bright as a bell. "Oh, come now, like you've never had a drink before. That's part of it, isn't it?"

"That much?" asked Jonas doubtfully.

"I have to get through the nights somehow," Sophie replied, as if it were a matter of course.

Stumped, he turned his face back to her and saw her smile as she gazed at the waning moon. "Sounds more like work than pleasure," he said dryly.

"It's exhausting, true enough," Sophie admitted bluntly. "But it's not like I have a choice. Luca needs me."

Jonas groaned, "Sophie, you always have a choice."

"You mean by leaving Luca to the curse?" She shook her head. "No, Jonas, I can't do that to him. Not ever. Besides, it's fun, isn't it? A lot of fun. It's worth all the pain to me."

Every word was like a dagger thrust into his guts. He didn't like how Luca had her wrapped around his finger with his curse story. He was still convinced the dancer was one of those pricks that amused themselves at the expense of young girls.

"Then why all the alcohol?" he asked.

"That's part of it," Sophie laughed. "Besides, Tomas always mixes me a special drink. It tastes so delicious you wouldn't believe it."

Jonas wouldn't have touched something Tomas had mixed if he were paid for it.

Before he could retort, however, Sophie had come to a realisation. "You know, Jonas? You're always so terribly serious. Everything has to go according to plan and make sense. You're always searching for some higher goal in your life, as if that matters. Why don't you just live?"

Jonas' steps faltered. He stared at Sophie in puzzlement. But she only smiled at him in a drunken stupor, not a hint of reproach in her eyes. Merely well-intentioned advice for a friend. How would she know that he had long since given up hope of a normal life?

With a sigh, Jonas rested his forehead on hers and came much closer to her lips than he could bear. "Oh, Sophie, don't you know you're all the life I need?"

—

Sophie hadn't even eaten breakfast, almost falling asleep in his arms. Jonas had put her to bed and was now tidying up the flat before he went to do the week's shopping. Her words were still in his head as he racked his brains over whether he should tell Sophie's father about his daughter's excessive drinking.

As if it's any of your business. Sighing, Jonas leaned against the dresser. Sophie was an adult. If she wanted to get drunk every night, that was her call. Whether or not he believed in it, the curse was real to her, and as long as she took it seriously, she would go to The DeModie every night, and there was nothing Jonas could do about it. No matter how much he wished he could.

Frustrated, he bent down to pick up the pointe shoes and stroked the broken satin fabric, lost in thought. How she could dance in these shoes was a complete mystery to him. No wonder her feet hurt all the time.

Carefully, Jonas put the shoes on the dresser and reached for his jacket, then left the house. The thought of Sophie and her broken shoes accompanied him. He couldn't stop repeating and dissecting her words in his head.

Sophie was having fun with Luca, but the constant strain was beginning to have consequences. Every day, the night, and therefore the time she had to dance with Luca, became longer. It was the fact she was putting her own life on hold for her supposed prince that displeased Jonas the most.

She'd told him that he should just live, but Jonas hadn't known what to do with his life for a long time. He had no needs, no desires, and certainly no dreams, anymore. The best he could hope for was that the nightmares would leave him alone one day. For that reason, Sophie's sheer joy at being alive and the dream she no longer dared to dream were almost sacred to him.

Perhaps that was why he stopped in front of the small ballet shop downtown. The music inside brought back memories. It was one of the songs he had often heard in Sophie's studio back in late summer, when she was still training daily. If he closed his eyes, he could see her spinning in circles, her free leg and arms stretched high in the air.

As he let his eyes wander over the displays, he spotted a mother with her two daughters looking at tutus. A smile crossed his lips when Jonas saw their enthusiasm. He could easily imagine Sophie visiting this shop with her mother and picking out a new tulle skirt.

Just a few days ago, he had received another payment and hadn't known what to buy with the rest left after he'd paid his living costs. No film, book, or game appealed to him, and even though he didn't have a wardrobe as lavish as Sophie's, the things he owned were enough for him. Now, he finally had an idea.

If he couldn't treat himself, maybe he could treat Sophie instead.

⁓

"You're out of your mind," Sophie muttered, a week later. Surrounded by children and their parents, they stood outside the big theatre in the early afternoon, waiting to be let in. "Tickets to the winter ballet. My father is clearly paying you too much."

Smirking, Jonas replied, "Can't I show my appreciation for you letting me stay with you with a little gesture?" The weather left much to be desired, but Jonas couldn't have been happier. Sophie had dressed up for their afternoon together. Her hair was elegantly pinned up and her face discreetly made up. She had also hooked an arm under his, looking for warmth.

"Well, in theory, it was my father who gave you the keys," Sophie said evasively. "I wouldn't even know how to repay you for this." Despite her words, he could sense her nervousness as the doors finally opened.

Slowly, people began to move, and they drifted towards the entrance. "Not at all. We're friends. I wanted to treat you, that's all," Jonas suggested, pulling out his tickets.

Her smile was everything to him. "Thank you," she whispered. Her excitement drove away all objections as they entered the foyer with its high ceiling. Sophie stared up, completely entranced.

Curious, Jonas followed her gaze and admired the detailed frescoes depicting scenes from Greek mythology. Several columns, modelled after ancient temples, supported the balcony with its elaborate balustrades. A chandelier hung from the ceiling, its crystals sending thousands of light spots dancing across the floor.

"Shall I take your coat?" Jonas asked quietly, so he wouldn't startle Sophie. Lost in thought, she took off her coat and let it fall into his arms. With a content smile, Jonas carried the clothes to the coat-room. His surprise was successful beyond his wildest dreams.

When he returned, Sophie turned to him with shining eyes. "I forgot how beautiful it is." A chime rang through the air, and Jonas felt his own excitement rising. "Come on, I want to see if our seats are any good!" She grabbed his hand and pulled him towards the large double doors.

The stalls had already been sold out, but Jonas had managed to get tickets in the first row of the balcony. They weren't the best seats, but Sophie didn't seem to mind. She took a seat next to him and immediately leaned her arms on the railing, as if she could see more of the empty stage that way. While the other guests found their way to their seats, she excitedly told him where the entrances were backstage, what pieces had probably been chosen for this year's winter ballet, and what details he should pay attention to.

Finally, the bell rang three times, and the lights went out one by one. Sophie seemed to hold her breath while the rest of the hall fell silent. The first sounds rang out softly, carrying Jonas away with them. Although he immediately recognised the first piece from Sophie's training sessions, the orchestra made it sound ten times as opulent. Then the dancers entered the stage and began to tell their story.

Completely spellbound, Jonas sat and watched the elegant movements portraying grand emotions and exciting developments without any words. He effortlessly followed the individual stories and was fascinated each time by how diverse the dances were, despite the limited figures.

Although some of the children squealed from time to time, Jonas didn't take his eyes off the stage once. But then, he heard a choked gasp beside him. Irritated, he turned his face away from the stage. Sophie had put her hand to her mouth, tears running down her cheeks as she kept sniffling. Startled, she noticed his gaze and jumped up on the spot.

"Soph..." he half-cried, hurrying after her, not minding the complaints around them.

As he stepped onto the balcony outside, he saw Sophie run down the stairs and rush out the door.

"Damn it!" Jonas didn't even have time to get their coats as he hurried after her.

Luckily for him, Sophie had stopped outside. Trembling, she was bending forward, clutching her mid-section.

Concerned, Jonas stepped closer and reached out to her. "Is something wrong?"

"Is something wrong?" Shrill, her voice rang across the empty courtyard as she jerked her head up. Her face was tear streaked. "You drag me to a ballet, of all things, and you want to know if something is *wrong*?"

Confused, Jonas tried to make sense of her words. "But you were enjoying it until just now. I saw the gleam in your eyes."

"I hate ballet! I hate it!" she screamed, pounding her fists on his chest.

Jonas stumbled back in surprise at her sudden attack.

"But you just had to bring me here," she continued to shout, then turned away again with a frustrated yelp. New sobs broke out and Jonas could see her wiping her wet cheeks again and again.

"Sophie," he began tentatively.

"She died during a performance." Sophie fanned her face, trying to stop the tears from falling. She turned back to him, her eyes full of helplessness. "My mother. She died during my performance as the Sugar Plum Fairy. You didn't think about that, did you?" It had been the dance of the Sugar Plum Fairy when they'd left the theatre.

Completely overwhelmed, Jonas found no answer. Sophie wiped tears from the corners of her eyes again before looking at her watch. "I have to go. Luca's waiting."

The words struck him like a slap. "Sure," he replied in a toneless whisper, lowering his gaze. "I'll get our coats."

—

Sophie had long since left the house, while Jonas was still grappling with the events of the afternoon. He'd wanted to make her happy. It had all started so well. Her excitement had infected him and the gleam in her eyes had told him all he needed to know about her love of ballet. How was he supposed to know that her mother had died in a theatre, of all places? While Sophie was on stage?

Jonas tossed the thought back and forth, but he couldn't figure out how he could've avoided that disaster. Just like he had no idea how to make amends. There was no mistaking that the matter had upset her greatly. After all, she had rushed to The DeModie long before sunset, leaving him behind.

It was no use. He could lie awake all night, wondering what exactly he'd done wrong. Or he could go after Sophie and apologise to her. Without further ado, Jonas took the old coat he had received from the beggar and set off.

Dusk had already set in, but the Niemeyer Street still lay deserted. It was too early in the evening for most partygoers, but not for Sophie. For twenty minutes, Jonas waited in his coat outside The DeModie for someone to appear so he could enter along with them. Then he lost patience.

He crossed the street and tried the door handle. Either the coat had other undreamed-of powers or he had something akin to fortune on this unfortunate day, for the door opened without a hitch. There was no sign of Tomas, although music was already blaring from downstairs. Shrugging his shoulders, Jonas entered the club.

While he was still puzzling over why The DeModie had no bouncer today, he began his descent through the gold and silver forest. The tinkling of the leaves was as enchanting as before, but now and then discordant sounds crept in, as if the chimes had been damaged.

Halfway up, Jonas stopped and looked down at the lake. Unlike last time, Sophie and Luca were the only ones dancing. On the shore, however, people crowded around, their attention focused on the couple. Jonas could understand their fascination only too well. In Luca's arms, Sophie floated across the dance floor. Instead of the fast rhythms from last time, the DJ had put on quieter music, a waltz or something like it. Sophie's gaze never left Luca's face.

The sight of her stung Jonas' heart. He should've known better, but he'd fallen head over heels for the fun-loving dancer. The smile, which seemed to light up the entire room, however, belonged entirely to her prince.

As before, Luca was an inexhaustible source of politeness and elegance. He let Sophie shine while he led her through the dance with a strong hand. Every step was spot on, and he twirled Sophie around and lifted her into the air with ease. The sight put the afternoon's magic to shame.

Jonas didn't know how long he'd watched them, when Luca bowed and breathed a kiss on Sophie's fingers. "The sight of you enchants me every night," he murmured to Sophie, and yet his words echoed in every corner of the room. When Jonas saw the happiness reflected in Sophie's face, his stomach turned.

Luca was perfect. He was good-looking, could dance brilliantly, and flitted around Sophie like a colourful butterfly. Always helpful, always obliging. Basking in his attention, it was clear why Sophie only had eyes for him and would grant him his peculiar wish of dancing with him for a year.

Once again, the couple glided across the mirrored dance floor, astonishing their admirers. Jonas wanted to hate Luca for his elegance and infallibility. He was almost consumed with finding some kind of detail that was wrong with him, around which he could spin the rest. Jealousy urged him to report to Sophie's father that his daughter had fallen in with a cheat, so he would forbid her from ever entering the club again, but Luca treated Sophie impeccably. The young man never mis-stepped, never faltered. And judging by his demeanour, he could well have belonged to an old royal house. No wonder Sophie fell for him lock, stock, and barrel, and could hardly take her eyes off him, while she never really noticed Jonas.

He should have been glad that she had someone who made her this happy. Someone who was living life to the fullest, not stuck hour after hour in some long-gone war. But whichever way he looked at it, envy wouldn't allow it. Like a moth to the flame, Sophie drew him in, and although there was nothing for him to gain, he couldn't let go of her. In no time at all, Sophie had become the centre of his miserable life.

Looking around, Jonas was startled to realise he wasn't the only one pining for Sophie. The people on the shore had their eyes fixed on the pretty dancer. In their eyes, he saw a hunger that reminded him of his own. As if they too were craving her flickering light.

Irritated by this observation, Jonas made his way around the room. Most of the people present were spellbound by what was happening on the dance floor. As other guests came down the stairs, the spell that had captivated the whole of The DeModie was fading bit by bit.

Amazed, he recognised the bouncer on bar duty today. He was serving a woman a disgustingly blue drink. "Oh, Sina, you should be getting used to it by now," Jonas heard him say in a pitying tone that didn't fit his previous experience with him.

The woman sobbed out loud. "You don't understand, Tomas! I can't just stand by and do nothing."

Tomas shrugged, and for a moment, his gaze slid longingly to the dance floor. "You don't have a choice. That's the way it's always been, and that's the way it'll always be. The only hope we have is that one day it will be our turn. Maybe there'll even be a second chance for you."

Sina burst into tears at his words, and Tomas stroked her hand compassionately, a stark contrast to the murderous looks he'd given Jonas.

Jonas decided not to eavesdrop on them any longer and crept around the room like a shadow to observe the other guests. He was convinced now that the cloak made him completely invisible, though he couldn't fathom how that was possible. At least, this way, he didn't have to worry about attracting attention.

"It's just as dark outside as it is in here. It's not worth it," a horse-faced man remarked nearby.

When his counterpart opened his mouth, Jonas was startled by yellow and crooked teeth that resembled tusks. "Bad enough we have to watch the princes punch their ticket to the surface. Now you don't even want to get fresh air at night?"

With a sinking feeling, Jonas remembered the people who'd been hanging around the club outside lately and the shadows Sophie was afraid of.

Was Luca's story true? The fact that the other visitors to the club—or were they residents?—were talking about princes as well irritated Jonas. He looked back at the dance floor. Next to

Sophie, three young women were dancing with men that were as outrageously good-looking as Luca, like the fairy-tale princes some little girls and women dreamed of.

Now that he was on the lookout for them, Jonas noticed how horrible the people on the shoreline looked in comparison. He'd be wary to meet most of them alone in a dark alley. There were unsightly humps, ugly scars, crooked teeth and noses, mismatched pairs of eyes and ugly warts. Occasionally, he saw people whose only flaw was a lack of shoes. More than anyone else, they fluctuated between an irrepressible longing and deep sadness.

As superficial as it was, considering this crowd, Luca really seemed like an enchanted prince held here against his will. But why that was, Jonas couldn't figure out. He considered whether the curse could still be a lie. If it was, Jonas liked the whole deal even less now that he knew what Sophie was exposed to each night.

After a while, a man caught Jonas' eye. Sitting alone in a boat, he was the only one whose gaze wasn't one of unfulfilled longing. With bloodshot eyes, the stranger followed Sophie's and Luca's movements, his face a distorted mask of rage. Cautiously, Jonas crept closer, fearful that the cloak would not protect him from this man, but the stranger never let his gaze stray from Sophie.

Jonas thought he could well be Luca's older brother with his blue eyes, blond hair, and sinewy body. But unlike the other young men, he wasn't dancing, just minding his drink. It was the same blue drink Tomas had offered the woman, and despite the early hour, it didn't seem to be his first.

Out of the corner of his eye, Jonas saw Luca leading Sophie to another boat, joking and flirting. It was in stark contrast to the stranger who was clawing his fingers into the wood of the table, leaving behind deep furrows. Jonas was startled when he realised what he was seeing. He wanted to believe it was a defect in workmanship or a natural sheaf on the board, but even as he watched, his fingernails dug deeper into the wood.

Jonas fought down his panic with great difficulty, keeping his breath shallow so as not to give himself away. While Sophie and Luca took their seats not far from them, the stranger finished his cocktail. His fingers tightened around the glass. A moment later, the vessel shattered. Sophie startled, glancing their way, while Jonas drew in a hissing breath.

As if from nowhere, Tomas appeared, slid past him and set a new drink down in front of the man. "Pull yourself together, Frederick! You'll only get into trouble again," he chastised him, almost caringly.

In response, the bartender had the broken glass hurled at his face. Sharp edges cut the even skin, and Tomas reflexively squeezed his eyes shut. "Go back to your bar, Tommy, and leave me alone!"

There it was again. The murderous look that had terrified Jonas so much. Hastily, Tomas bowed his head, feigning an apology, and turned away before Frederick could throw anything else after him. As he rushed past Jonas, the cuts were already closing on their own, as if sewn together by an invisible hand.

Jonas swallowed and staggered back. He had seen the blood. He still saw the traces of it on Tomas' shirt, but when the bouncer arrived back at his bar, the wounds had disappeared as if they'd never been there. Disgruntled, the young man continued to fill glasses.

Meanwhile, Jonas looked around frantically. Something was very wrong with The DeModie. He was more certain now than ever that he had to get Sophie out of here. Together with Luca, if necessary.

But first, he had to convince her of that. Disregarding his invisibility, Jonas pushed through the people towards the stairs. If they noticed him at all, their sinister greed for Sophie and the other girls was stronger. A few steps up, he paused and looked back. Sophie didn't seem to notice the many stares that followed her, even away from the dance floor. Instead, she laughed at Luca and let him shower her with kisses. Trembling, Jonas turned away. She wouldn't believe him. Not without proof.

After there had been such a loud crash last time, he was hesitant to step between the gold and silver trees. Beneath him, the filigree moss broke with a soft crunch, making his trail abundantly clear despite the cloak. With a last glance back, he braced himself and broke off one of the golden branches for proof.

The thunder was even more terrible this time. Jonas winced violently, fearing that the ceiling was about to collapse on him.

But only lightning flashed in the artificial sky, with a deep rumble in the distance. Dust as thick as clouds rose and began to envelop Jonas. The music sounded shrill and distorted in his ears, and then he saw figures coming towards him.

He knew exactly who these people were: Taliban who had ambushed his team.

They would shoot him, or worse, capture him. The coat wouldn't protect Jonas. Not in Afghanistan. Breathing frantically, he rushed towards two large shadows, running blindly through the clouds of dust rising from the bombed buildings.

Disjointed scraps of words reached him. Orders that made no sense, last words of comrades, never forgotten, and foreign words, of which he only understood one because he had heard it too often: *Help! Help!*

At last, Jonas found his way up the mountain. He was panting heavily and held his side with the hand that still clutched the golden branch. Behind him, ghastly gunshots rang out. Jonas threw himself to the ground in desperation. The moss burst beneath him, and thousands of tiny splinters bored into his skin. The pain drove him up again. Aimlessly, Jonas fled from the shadows in the mists, darting left and right until he had completely lost his bearings. The scar on his shoulder burned with pain, and his pulse throbbed in his ears. Still, he continued running until, all at once, he stopped, frozen in place.

In front of his eyes, a long ledge was attached to the wall. Countless nails had been hammered into the wood, and on each of them hung a pair of broken shoes. On some of them, the soles were coming off, while others were completely riddled with holes. Frayed laces hung down from a few, barely holding the shoes together. On many of them, the paint had faded or peeled off. Still others were encrusted with dirt down to the last inch.

In a ghastly trance, Jonas walked past the shoes and looked at each one of them. Often, they were once elegant dancing shoes, but every now and then he saw some practical boots. There were women's and men's shoes and, to his horror, even smaller ones that wouldn't have fitted Sophie's narrow feet if she tried. Just thinking about what that might mean made Jonas sick.

It seemed to him that for every resident of The DeModie, there was a hook with broken shoes. But the most horrible sight of all was the empty nail at the end of the ledge.

The place for Sophie's shoes.

Sauté

The bass vibrated in Sophie's veins while the beat directed her feet. Luca's strong arms gave her support as she bent backwards, almost touching the floor with her hands. Sophie closed her eyes and enjoyed the music. When she came back up, a yawn escaped her.

Luca stifled a laugh. "Am I that boring?"

"You'd be the last person I'd be bored with," she assured him, turning under his arm.

Luca had other plans and pulled her towards him. His arms wrapped around her waist and his chin came to rest on her shoulder. "Good."

Laughing, Sophie lifted her right arm and stroked the soft hairs on Luca's neck as she snuggled against him. A short moan escaped his lips, and a little later, she felt his hot breath on her neck.

Sophie was about to turn and intercept his next kiss when a loud crack threw her off balance.

Luca cried out and stumbled. "Damn it!" he cursed, drawing in a sharp breath.

Concerned, Sophie watched him as he leaned forward, breathing heavily. "Is everything okay?"

Once or twice, Luca took a deep breath, then he raised his head and smiled at her. "I'll be fine. I just twisted my ankle." Pain wiped the smile from his face again, and quickly Sophie reached under his arms to support him.

"Thanks." Instead of looking at her, however, Luca searched the club.

When Sophie did the same, she flinched violently. Horrified, she stumbled backwards. If Luca hadn't held her, she would've fallen to the floor. Her breath was catching in her throat, and everything was spinning around her.

"Sophie! What is it?" His words reached her through a thick haze.

"The people," she answered shakily, clinging to his arm. "Just look at the people!"

Her worst nightmares had suddenly come true, and this time no turning around or looking away helped. Very few of the guests resembled humans now. Instead, she saw enormous horns and sharp claws, thick fur and powerful tusks. Bared teeth gnashed menacingly and the greedy looks from their eyes caused her to break out in a cold sweat. The snorts and grunts of so many throats almost drowned out the music.

Anxiously, Sophie pressed closer to Luca and hid her face against his chest. "I'm scared," she admitted in a whisper.

Luca's fingers slipped under her chin, and he lifted her gaze. He alone was unchanged, his blue eyes full of love. They gave Sophie strength. Her breathing calmed a little, and the trembling subsided.

At last, Luca nodded and replied in perfect calm, "You see their true form." When she gasped, he added. "You don't have to be afraid, Sophie. They're still the same as before."

"They weren't as scary when they were human, though." Sophie knew she sounded pathetic, but she was tired, and the terror stuck deep in her bones. Add to that the drama of the afternoon with Jonas, which had brought up all those painful memories of her mother.

The exhaustion caused her to cry, prompting Luca to stroke her hair. "Nothing will happen to you as long as I'm here. No one will touch you."

His words began to lull her to safety. Slowly, his warmth calmed her. Her eyes fell shut.

"Hey." Gently, Luca woke her from the doze she had sunk into.

Somehow, her feet had continued to move along with the music. Tired, Sophie looked into Luca's amused eyes.

"Just say that you need a break." He broke away from her and took her hand.

The sudden coldness as he parted from her made Sophie a little more alert. Relieved, she followed him to their boat. As usual, it was reserved for them. Sophie sunk into the soft velvet cushions with a sigh. The tension left her body, and slowly, her eyelids became heavy again. While Luca raised his hand to draw Tomas' attention, she snuggled into his arm and dozed off.

"In a minute, Sophie, in a minute," Luca murmured, somewhat impatiently. She wondered if he was annoyed that she was no longer dancing with him, but it felt so good to rest her aching feet for a moment.

When she opened her eyes next, Tomas was leaning past her and set down a deep blue drink for her. "A double for our pretty princess. Enjoy!"

Puzzled, Sophie looked at the glass and at Tomas' waiting expression. Something was different from usual. Both brothers seemed tense, and Sophie had to think back to the noise from before. Had there been a problem with the music system or Bastien?

Luca picked up the glass for her and handed it to her. "We'll get you back up on your feet in no time," he said in good nature, though his face showed a hint of worry.

"Back on my feet?" Sophie just wanted to sleep a little in his arms, as she often did in Jonas' arms when he carried her home.

Tomas nodded and grinned mischievously. "It's my best cocktail. Nothing is more refreshing. I promise."

Sophie regarded Luca doubtfully. She didn't like the way the smile didn't reach his eyes and the fingers of his other hand drummed nervously on his knee. "Go ahead and drink. It will do you good. Or would you rather go home?" The edge in his voice was hard to miss.

She got it now. He was scared. Sleeping was not an option. Not until the year was up and they had completed their last dance at dawn.

Sighing, Sophie straightened again. She suspected there was more to the cocktail than the two brothers were telling her. But she was also convinced that Luca wouldn't slip her anything dangerous and raised the glass to her mouth.

Tomas had told the truth. As soon as the first drop touched her throat, a wonderful, fruity sweetness with hints of honey spread through her mouth. No sooner had she taken the first sip than she perceived every single note of The DeModie's intoxicating melody. A comforting warmth permeated every fibre of her body, making her nerves tingle.

"What is this?" Sophie asked Tomas in wonder, only barely maintaining enough restraint not to drink the wondrous beverage in one go.

Grinning, Tomas replied, "The tears of my hard work."

Giggling, Sophie put the glass back to her lips and feasted on the taste and the wondrous feeling that spread inside of her. Even the pain in her feet gave way to the lovely sweetness. Amused, Sophie noticed that her heart was now beating to the rhythm of the music.

When Luca looked at her expectantly, Sophie laughed and took his hands, ready to surrender to the unearthly beautiful sounds again. He, too, was beaming at her. Gone were the worry and tension she had imagined in her tiredness.

The figures on the dance floor no longer seemed scary to Sophie. They might look menacing with their claws and tusks, but they knew how to turn every night into day just as well as before. In keeping with her mood, Bastien put on something fast and lively. Whooping, Sophie let Luca spin her in circles until she felt dizzy.

Closer than ever, her admirers pressed, and several times Luca had to ask for them to give them some space.

Sophie didn't care. The DeModie was a place of dancing, after all, and if she had wanted to be on stage with only her partner, she would have stuck to ballet. Flustered, she clicked her tongue. "Let them join in! The more the merrier."

Her wonderful prince looked at her with concern. "Are you sure, Sophie?" When she nodded, his features softened, and a dreamy glint entered his eyes. "You have no idea how happy you make me." He raised her hands to his lips and kissed her fingers. "And them, too."

Again, Sophie had to giggle. Her tiredness was wiped away. "Well, isn't that what princesses do? Care for the people?"

Before she knew it, she felt Luca's lips on hers. His kiss tasted as sweet as the cocktail she'd drunk. Swooning, Sophie put her arms around his neck and pulled him closer.

Something tugged her neck, and Sophie gasped in surprise. Luca withdrew his hand and brought it forward. A reddish haze swirled around his fingers. With a smile to her, he tossed the haze into the crowd. Sophie watched in wonder as the others lapped it up, as if Luca had just declared the buffet open. It was her zest for life they lusted for, Sophie noted, not without pride.

A little later, the people seemed more balanced than before. Their eyes shone with contentment, and all because of her. *So, this is what it feels like to be a princess,* Sophie thought in a daze. *Someone who sacrifices themselves for their people's happiness.*

Laughing, Sophie spun in circles. Luca's touch made her skin tingle pleasantly as he spread more and more of her joy into the crowd. And why shouldn't they have some of what she had? She had the best life she could wish for. A ball every night, friends who understood her, and a prince of her own who fulfilled her every wish.

She couldn't get enough of Luca. His blond hair, his loving blue eyes. He was as if he'd stepped out of a storybook. His strong hand guided her through each song, and Sophie was convinced he could wield a sword as well as he danced, if necessity ever forced him to.

Of all the princes in the room, Sophie had been picked by the most beautiful and wonderful. Tomas, with his boyish charm, was far too young, even if she had grown to like him like a little brother of her own. He would only be entitled to a princess when the older ones had found theirs. Until then, he would dutifully serve his brothers.

Bastien, the wonderful Master of Music, was still too childish for her taste. Far too often, he made fun of her and Luca or teased Tomas. But the magic he performed every evening at the mixing desk had secured him a place in Sophie's heart. No one could make her dance as beautifully as he could.

She liked every single one of them, the older ones as well as the younger ones, and she would have loved to set them all free. All but one.

Frederick still creeped her out. Despite the wonderful lightness of the music and sweetness of Tomas' drink, he sat in his boat from dusk until dawn. A few weeks ago, Sophie had felt sorry for him because Pia had dumped him, but since Luca had won the dance battle, Frederick had been consumed with envy. Because of his age, he was convinced that Sophie should be his by right. As if she were nothing more than a possession and could be handed from one to the other.

Jonas had once mused aloud that Sophie was as interchangeable for Luca, if the curse was true; that she was nothing more to him than a ticket to the surface. But when she looked into Luca's eyes, she knew that couldn't possibly be true. Their love was what she had always dreamed of: the only true one, worth facing all hardships.

The intoxicating effect of Tomas' drink lasted for the rest of the night, and Sophie danced in tune with the music until dawn. A feeling of blissful inertia overcame her when she finally left the club. She hardly noticed that Jonas threw a coat around her, just as she hadn't noticed the rain pattering on her bare skin before. She didn't even feel the chill of the late November day, though there was frost on every surface.

None of Jonas' horrified comments got through to her. They meant little compared to the exhilaration of her enchanted world. Even the firm grip with which he kept Sophie from slipping on the wet floor was much more bearable than usual. He was just worrying unnecessarily, as usual.

"Come on, at least pull yourself together for a bit," Jonas begged her.

Sophie couldn't help but laugh. She wanted to spin in circles with him. "Dance, Jonas! Dance! You're always so terribly stiff and brooding. A little exercise would do you good."

Jonas held her close, his brows furrowed deeply. "Gee, Sophie, your father's here!"

Chuckling, she turned, almost toppling to one side if Jonas hadn't kept a firm grip on her. She couldn't spot her father anywhere on the empty, wet street. "Where is he?"

"Not here, at home. He's waiting there for us," Jonas said as if it were the first sign of the end of the world.

Again, Sophie had to laugh. The way he almost despaired because of her just looked too droll. "What's he doing there? Doesn't he have to go to work?"

"It's Sunday!" Jonas said angrily. "The first advent Sunday." She hadn't paid attention to any weekdays or holidays since she'd started dancing with Luca. What did they matter anymore?

Frustrated, Jonas gave up trying to talk to her. With a tight face, he trudged home. His eternally grumpy mood, however, was bouncing off her today. "Why don't we just go to the park?" She would love to show him all the places she had grown up in.

Inevitably, he groaned. "Sophie, it's raining. Besides, you have to get home." Murmuring, he added, "And to bed."

Sophie rolled her eyes. It was always the same. He'd pick her up, take her straight home and tuck her into bed. When she woke up, he'd provide her with a hearty breakfast and take her back to The DeModie. Jonas needed these routines, unable to let loose. And because Sophie liked him, she indulged him. But it bored her to death.

After all, she'd never run into her shadowy pursuers.

Smirking, Sophie endured his silence until they were at her door. Jonas unlocked it with a shaky hand, as if something horrible lurked in her apartment. He was probably seeing things again that she couldn't perceive. Something from the war.

But when the door opened, there was only her father sitting in the living room, his face full of reproach. All at once, the music in her head faded, and she felt the cold in her hair. Jonas was worse off, since he wasn't even wearing a coat. His blue woollen jumper was completely soaked, and his lips quivered with cold. Stoically, he kept his composure. He looked as if he was about to salute her father.

Downright ridiculous.

Only then did Sophie realise that she was wearing his coat. She took it off and handed it back to him.

"And where is your coat, Sophie?" Her father's imperious tone made Sophie wince. At the same time, defiance stirred inside her. She didn't have to put up with such things anymore.

Shrugging, Sophie answered, "I forgot it."

Her father's brow furrowed deeply. Then his gaze fell on Jonas. "Dismissed." Like the good soldier he was, Jonas obeyed on the spot, vanishing into his room.

Meanwhile, her father came to her and regarded her closely. Instantly, she became aware that she was wearing nothing more than a half-drenched dance dress.

"Did you take drugs?"

"Dad!" Sophie exclaimed in horror. Typical his thoughts would go there.

"Don't look at me like that! Your pupils are dilated, your cheeks red. You look thin." When she began to roll her eyes, he relented a little. "Gee, kid, I'm just worried about you. I hardly get to see you, and having you arrive here in that get-up..."

Offended, Sophie folded her arms in front of her chest. "I've been dancing, Dad. You know, the thing people do when they want to have fun."

"With your boyfriend?" her father asked, as if he hadn't heard her objection. So, Jonas had blabbed to him, after all. What else did she expect from the obedient soldier?

Frustrated, Sophie threw her hands up in the air and then placed them on her hips. "Is this going to be an interrogation?" She felt betrayed and no longer in the mood to be gracious.

"Is there any other way to hear from you?" The accusation followed right on her heels.

For a moment, they glared at each other in silence. In time, her father's features softened a little. "You're my everything. You know that."

Sophie couldn't stand it anymore. "Really? You're just like Jonas! You think just because you care and worry about me, you get to tell me how to live my life."

She didn't care that her father took a step back, hiding his feelings behind the rigid officer's mask he wore so often. "I'm not telling you what to do. I just wish you would finally do something meaningful with your life."

"But I love dancing," Sophie exclaimed as tears welled up in her eyes. "It makes me happy, and I don't want to do anything else. Just dance! Every day and every night. With Luca, I can do exactly that. He's the only one who doesn't have unfulfillable expectations of me."

"Unfulfillable, such as earning your own money?" her father asked.

The answer took her breath away. She was too exhausted to argue with him, too tired to listen to his reproaches. "I could make money dancing, but that wouldn't be good enough for you. You're never satisfied with me," Sophie accused him, defiantly wiping the tears from her cheeks.

Her father sighed heavily. He always did that when he thought she was acting childish. "Sophie, I know you love dancing, and for all I care, go, dance! But not in a nightclub. This is all about partying and drinking. Or is there a pole dancing career I don't know about?"

Sophie gasped, shocked that he dared say that.

Her father rubbed the bridge of his nose as he continued a little more conciliatory, "Besides, Jonas says you've gotten yourself entangled with some kind of cult there."

Besides, Jonas says... The words burned themselves into her soul. So that was why he was here. Jonas had betrayed her trust after she had run away from the theatre yesterday. Obviously, he couldn't help reporting to his commander. And she'd trusted him. Had even trusted him with her old dreams for the future.

"Is that true, Sophie?" Her father's voice snapped her out of her thoughts again. "Or are you not even talking to me now?" The expression on her father's face made her uncomfortable. She had never known him this vulnerable.

All at once, she longed for her bed. Her father would never understand why she had agreed to help Luca. "It's not a cult."

"But?" The way he raised his eyebrows made Sophie angry again.

"It's a normal dance club. People have fun there. But that's probably incomprehensible to you and Jonas." Her father sighed heavily. She had to be quick if she were to gain the upper hand. "Is it true you hired Jonas to spy on me?"

Now he frowned. "What makes you think that? Jonas works for the company."

Sophie nervously brushed a strand of hair from her face before crossing her arms. "Then he didn't tell you where I go every night?"

Her father couldn't lie any better than Jonas could. "That was once."

"Twice," she corrected him gruffly. "I know you support me financially and I live here under your roof, but that doesn't give you the right to have me shadowed 24/7." She hesitated for only a brief moment before playing her last card. "If you think I'm nothing but a leech, I might as well move in with Luca. He'd take me in for sure and wouldn't pry into my affairs."

The trump card had a visible effect. Her father sharply drew in his breath. He said nothing for a while, then looked at her in dismay. "Do you want me to dismiss Jonas?" Sophie knew he was serious. Four weeks before Christmas, he would put Jonas out on the street, just for her sake.

Sophie was still so hurt about the betrayal that she considered it for a moment. Never again would she have to let Jonas mother her or endure his longing looks. But then she'd take everything he had. He'd mentioned that she was the only good thing in his life. How could she ever seriously consider pushing him away? And if she were true to herself, the looks even flattered her. If only they weren't as hungry as those of the creatures in The DeModie. Hungry for her life force.

Sophie shook her head. "No, I don't want that," she admitted quietly. She could never forgive herself. "He isn't a part of this. I just don't want him reporting every little thing I do to you."

Her father snorted. "Every little thing? That was the first time he ever came to me of his own accord. Normally, he won't even tell me if you even still lived here."

But Jonas had gone to him of his own accord. Only because Sophie had a breakdown in front of the theatre. With difficulty, she swallowed her anger and replied, "I'm still alive. Thank you for asking."

"But I don't like what you're doing. Dancing with that boy." Her father took another step forward and tried to take her hands in his, but Sophie pulled them away and backed away against the door. He sighed again. "I know these men, Sophie. They promise you the blue sky and get you drunk every night. And you drink because they pay, and you don't even realise how dependent you are on their attention. Or how it's slowly ruining your life."

It was too much. In her anger, she gasped for air like a fish out of water. "Luca isn't like that. He's a prince." Her passionate words only led to a pitying look from her father. Apparently, she was behaving childishly again. "A gentleman, if you prefer. He loves me more than anyone."

The words hurt him, but Sophie didn't care at that moment. She was tired of never being enough for her father. First, he didn't want her to dance ballet, and now he didn't want her to see Luca again. Her throat tightened with fear that he might actually follow through with his threats.

Something of that must have got through to him, because suddenly her father became lamb-like. "That's not true, Sophie. You should know that you are more important to me than anything else in the world."

Defiantly, she crossed her arms in front of her chest again. She couldn't let him get to her. Not if she wanted to keep Luca. He needed her so much, much more than her father did. "Then why can't I live my life the way I want? Trying things and failing like everyone else? I don't want to be a bird in a gilded cage just because you're too afraid I might break my wings."

She'd done it. Her father had tears in his eyes. The unfamiliar sight made her slightly nervous. Him, too, apparently, because he pulled his nose up briefly, blinked a few times, and looked at the clothes rack in the corner.

When he looked back at her, he had himself under control again. "Okay."

"Okay?" asked Sophie, dumbfounded.

"I'll stop pestering you." He obviously struggled with the concession. "It's no use, after all. You're going to do it your way and there's nothing I can do but watch." She'd never experienced him as meek as this. Her father never gave in. "But if you need help, Sophie, you'll come to me, won't you?"

Overwhelmed, Sophie could only nod. "Yes, of course. You're my dad."

Her reply brought a small smile to his lips. To her great relief, he took his coat after that. "Maybe you'll introduce me to your Luca some time."

She couldn't help but roll her eyes. Once again, he was trying to control her. At the same time, she realised that even this simple thing wasn't possible. Not until she'd broken Luca's curse. "Maybe in the summer." Until then, Luca was hers alone.

Her father nodded, even though she could see his disappointment. Then he came to her and hugged her tightly. "Check in once in a while," he whispered into her ear. Then he put on his hat and went out into the rain.

Sophie breathed a sigh of relief. She had made it through the confrontation. Luca was still safe.

When she heard Jonas' bedroom door open, her anger returned in a flash. "You have some nerve," she snapped at him.

Immediately, Jonas lowered his head. "I'm sorry I informed your father, but I didn't know what else to do."

"About what?" asked Sophie, horrified. "Where do you get the audacity to interfere with my life, anyway?"

As he looked down at his fingers, she thought he was going to give in as usual, but then he raised his chin with a pained expression. "Because I care about you, Sophie. And because I see you wearing yourself thin every night. Your feet hurt. You sleep all day. Your whole life revolves around dancing at The DeModie. Don't you realise you're just as cursed as he is?"

Annoyed, Sophie noticed her anger evaporating at the words. Jonas deserved her wrath, but because he already appeared in front of her like a beaten dog, she couldn't stay angry with him. "Oh, Jonas. I'm not cursed just because I'm trying to free Luca. I explained this to you. The whole thing about the year and the day. And sure, it's exhausting, but it's also nice at The DeModie. The atmosphere, the music, Luca."

Jonas' mouth twisted in frustration. "You mean that wonderful atmosphere of slathering perverts crowding around you and looking like they want to eat you? Or do you mean the people who split wood with their bare hands or whose wounds can heal in seconds?"

Shocked, Sophie looked at him. "What are you talking about? That sounds like a very wild dream to me, Jonas," she tried to ease his concerns. Nevertheless, she tightened her arms around the middle of her body. The words reminded her of the hunger and now, without the wonderful drink in her body, the residents of The DeModie seemed scary again.

"I was there, Sophie!" exclaimed Jonas, slightly annoyed. Before she could react, he disappeared into his room.

Irritated, Sophie stared after him and wondered if she shouldn't just go to bed. She was too tired to deal with Jonas' irritating behaviour now. Her feet longed for rest.

She had already half turned around when she decided to give in. One of them had to be an adult, after all, and as much as he annoyed her sometimes, she didn't want to scare away the last friend she had left outside of The DeModie.

His room was just as bare and tidy as she had expected it to be. Apart from his drawing pad, there was not a single thing of personal value. No pictures, no keepsakes, just fastidious tidiness. Even his things were still neatly stowed away in the travel bag instead of filling the cupboards. Nothing bore witness to the fact that a human being lived here. He could move out at a moment's notice and not a trace of him would remain.

Jonas, however, hadn't just left her standing. He was looking for something. And when he turned to Sophie, he had a surprise in store for her. In his hand, he held two twigs. One silver, the other gold. Their origin was obvious.

"You followed me?" she asked shakily.

He nodded uneasily. "In a way. The first time I was in, I was just curious. Someone had told me about The DeModie before I met you. He told me about all the treasures you could find there, and I wanted to see if it was true. And you went in there."

Horrified, Sophie took a few steps back. "You stole them? To enrich yourself?" The crack of thunder that had shaken The DeModie twice came to her mind.

"No," Jonas said vehemently. "I took them as evidence. No one would believe what I saw otherwise. The club is practically invisible. It's downright scary. But I was there. I saw you and Luca," he began to explain.

Her anger rekindled, Sophie interrupted him, "You saw Luca. And? Is he the monster you think he is?"

With a snort, Jonas shook his head. "I don't think he's a monster." There was that sadness in his eyes again that she could hardly bear. "Luca's perfect. He's good looking. He can dance like hell. And he's nice and accommodating."

His words took Sophie's breath away. As much as he liked her, she had expected sheer jealousy.

"But Luca isn't the problem," Jonas continued, his voice noticeably firmer. "Even if I don't like the story he told you to tie you to him. That club is dangerous."

Sophie had to laugh out loud. "Oh really? I told you it was the underworld, the place of demons and lost souls."

Jonas drew a breath in exasperation. "Then why are you going there?"

"Because I have to free Luca," Sophie repeated. What was so hard to understand about that?

Jonas was not so easily dissuaded and stepped closer. "But you're risking everything for him. Those people there... those lost souls or demons mean you no good. Did you see the looks on their faces?" He stood in front of her and swallowed. "They give me the creeps."

"Me too," Sophie admitted conciliatorily. Then she took Jonas' hands and squeezed them. "But Luca protects me. When he's there, they can't hurt me."

"And if he's not there?" asked Jonas, unwilling to trust her.

Releasing his hands, Sophie replied, "He's always there. Besides, his brothers keep an eye on me as well."

She'd said the wrong thing, for Jonas screwed up his face. "His brothers, the bouncer or bartender, or whatever he is, and the other pretty boys? I trust them even less."

"Princes, they are princes," Sophie corrected him, with growing unease.

Jonas nodded slightly. "You don't see them the way I do. The look the bouncer gave me would have sent shivers down your spine."

"Tomas is a sweet boy," she protested. Once again, Jonas's protective urge became exhausting.

Again, he snorted. "Yeah, right." But then he looked at her pleadingly, visibly struggling for words. "Please, Sophie. Let's find another solution."

Every word drained her substance. "I won't give up on Luca."

"I know you won't," Jonas said in desperation. "Listen. We'll go in there tomorrow night, and then we'll get Luca out. Even if I have to fight that Tomas and all the monsters of the underworld."

Sophie stared at him. "That's your solution? You're going to war for us?" Sheepishly, Jonas lowered his head, but Sophie could only snort in bewilderment. "Do you know what your problem is?"

Jonas swallowed.

"All you ever see is war. Only enemies all around you. I don't think you ever really came back from Afghanistan."

Balancé

Shots cut through the air and hit the wall behind Jonas. Debris fell and dust trickled down on him, taking his breath away. The smoke distorted the voices so much he didn't know if they were breathing down his neck or came from far away. Nor did he know if they were friend or foe.

"I'm going!" Sophie called out, momentarily snapping Jonas out of his memories. She looked tired, even though she'd made every effort to conceal the dark circles under her eyes with make-up. He knew better than to call her out on it. It wouldn't do any good, after all.

The slamming of the door catapulted him back into the war. Water was scarce, and they'd been walking in the mountains for days. The sun burned down on them, and his tongue tasted the dust. Jonas cast around tensely, since a Taliban could be lurking in any niche, no matter how small.

They were watching him, waiting for some carelessness that could be his undoing. The strain was beginning to show. At night, he could hardly sleep a wink. During the day, he lacked sleep. Nerves were frayed, orders became curt, and the mood was irritable.

Jonas was checking the crevices, which could easily accommodate a sniper, when a ring tone jolted him out of his thoughts. As if emerging from water, he slowly regained consciousness. His hands shook uncontrollably as he stared at them.

The ringing still pierced his ears until he finally understood that it came from his phone. With great difficulty, he raised his hand and reached for it. His mother. His fingers were shaking so badly the user interface alone was a challenge for him.

Then she was there. "...Jonas?" He had forgotten to answer. "Jonas, are you there?"

His words had disappeared. He knew he had to say something, but this simple, normal act was suddenly so foreign to him he no longer knew how to wring a sound from his body.

"Jonas?"

With some effort, he forced his tongue to form the letters. "Hello." As if that broke the spell, his head cleared, and the words came more easily. "Hey, how are you guys?" It was a good idea to take the focus away from the one question he couldn't answer.

The relief in his mother's voice as she sighed almost hurt. "Oh, quite well. Felix came home last week and introduced us to his girlfriend. The two of them have..." While his mother brought him up to speed, Jonas noticed himself drifting back into his memories from Afghanistan.

His hands were still shaking. As it wandered over to the liquor bottle and filled a glass, he felt as if he was just an observer to his life. It was only when the alcohol burned in his throat that he could muster the attention his mother demanded.

"They're planning to stay here until Christmas," she was telling him, and he already had an inkling of what was about to come. "And I was wondering when you were going to crash here?" Crash like bombs on the roofs of the hospital. "You are coming home, aren't you?"

The prospect of returning home terrified Jonas. He would have to answer questions. Questions about his livelihood, his future plans, his personal developments. None of which he could answer or wanted to deal with. Not in front of his family. After all, they all expected him to be fine. That he had his life under control.

"I don't think it's going to happen this year," Jonas heard himself lie. "I can't get away at the moment. You know, work and stuff." He had no idea what she had in mind when he talked about his work. He'd always been vague when asked about it.

Her disappointment was plain to hear. He had been making up similar excuses for well over a year. "At Christmas?"

He owed her a better explanation. "My boss has a lot on his plate. I can't leave now, I'm afraid. I'm sorry. I'll keep next year free." By then, he would come up with a new excuse.

"Jonas? Are you all right?" his mother asked all of a sudden.

He almost dropped the phone as the simple question made his heartbeat quicken and he recalled the trembling in his hands. Hastily, Jonas downed the rest of the shot glass and replied, "Yeah, sure. I'm just a little stressed. You know how it is."

"Hmm," she didn't sound convinced. Still, she let him get away with it. "I'm sure you're busy. Maybe you could come over in the new year, then. It could just be a weekend. Or an afternoon," she added softly.

He wanted so much to promise her, but he didn't dare. If he did, he would just find another reason not to go. "I'll see if something works out then."

Just like him, she feigned glee, as if she wasn't disappointed that they wouldn't see each other again any time soon. "Okay. Take care of yourself, will you?"

"Yes, Mum. And say hi to the others!" The false cheerfulness almost physically pained him. He quickly topped his glass up and downed the next shot so the burning would distract him.

He hung up and regarded the liquor bottle in shock. Only a small residue of clear liquid still covered the bottom. Jonas couldn't remember when he had drunk all the rest. Maybe when the Taliban had driven him out of bed or after the bomb had exploded.

Demonstratively, Jonas put the bottle in the cupboard. He had bought the alcohol on a whim after the visions had become stronger again. Drowning them in booze, however, had never been his intention. After all, that was Sophie's way of not having to face the loss of her mother. The alcohol and the dancing with Luca.

For a moment, he looked at the bottle, unable to close the door. "The last sip won't matter now," he murmured at last, and reached for it.

Since their argument, Sophie had insisted that he no longer accompany her to and from The DeModie. Jonas had given in and was rewarded with forgiveness. But not just that. For some reason, she made an effort to spend time with him on the weekends despite her late nights. He wasn't entirely comfortable with the arrangement, knowing how much her feet hurt and how tired she was at the end of the night. Yet, she was positively bubbling with life. By now, Jonas attributed this less to her zest for life than to the cocktails Luca gave her to keep her going through the ordeal. A theory he didn't dare share with Sophie after the last blow-up. Instead, they both pretended that there was nothing unusual about her nights at The DeModie.

"So, what do your parents want for Christmas?" asked Sophie, the excitement lighting up her eyes, as if she hadn't spent the entire night dancing. Or possibly, because of it.

"That's a very good question," Jonas replied. "My mother is pretty much happy with everything, my father with nothing."

Sophie laughed, bright as a bell. "That's not very helpful. Is there not even the slightest clue?"

Probably the only thing that would make them truly happy would be his presence. "Hmm, my mother likes decorative stuff. Lights, candles, soaps. My father likes books, preferably about history. Just hard to find something he doesn't already have." Besides, he had little desire to go through the departments where war pictures stared back at him from every other cover.

"Okay, then let's just go through the pedestrian zone and see what they have there. Maybe something will catch your eye," Sophie suggested, hooking her arm under his to gently guide him in the right direction.

As they walked down the street, Jonas noticed the many coloured lights in the windows. Although it was daytime, they promised warm, loving homes. Surely, his mother had also hung up her advent stars and lit up the garden with fairy lights. Longing tightened his throat, and he hastily averted his eyes.

"By the way, Dad says you're welcome to come over for Christmas lunch if you're not going home," Sophie suddenly said, as if she had read his thoughts.

Jonas eyed her in her thick coat and white earmuffs, her blonde hair peeking out from underneath. "Wouldn't that be strange?"

"Stranger than you and I living together? I'd love it if you were there and I didn't have to sit there alone with my dad," Sophie confided to him, winking. "Besides, you owe me."

Jonas raised an eyebrow. "I do?"

"Yes," Sophie replied, stretching the word so long it almost sounded as if it was sung. "You're to blame for the morning assault and fuelling his worry. Now you have to show him how much I've improved."

The infectious sparkle in her eyes told him she wasn't serious. Jonas frowned sceptically before he, too, had to grin. "Very well, if you need my support that much."

She stuck her tongue out at him. "Think of it as a Christmas bonus."

Shaking his head, Jonas followed her around the little Christmas market that occupied the pedestrian zone. Comfy huts with silvery glittering fake snow on the roofs offered countless treats and trinkets: gingerbread and grilled sausages, candles and wooden arches of lights, Christmas tree baubles, and children's toys. Christmas music sounded through the air, which was filled with the sweet, savoury, and spicy scents of Christmas.

It wasn't particularly busy yet, so they strolled leisurely from hut to hut, looking for little things for his parents and brother. "Look at this!" exclaimed Sophie ecstatically, as Jonas was having a porcelain lantern wrapped.

While stowing the small package in his backpack, he strolled over to the tinkling and singing stall Sophie had spotted. A whole armada of music boxes stood there ready to dance. To the left and right on the counter, two spun to a gentle melody.

Sophie opened a third music box. Enraptured, she watched the little ballerina with her raised leg as she elegantly spun in circles. She looked up with shining eyes as Jonas stepped next to her. "Isn't it beautiful? My mother used to have one just like it, and I remember watching it for hours. I don't even know what happened to it."

"Maybe it's buried in some corner under your clothes," Jonas teased, and Sophie's mouth dropped open in indignation. Cheerfully, he waved the salesman over.

Confused, Sophie frowned. "You're not going to buy something for me again, are you?"

Grinning, Jonas motioned the salesman to wrap the music box up. "Think of it as a Christmas bonus."

Sophie nudged him in the side with her elbow, but Jonas could see the blissful twinkle in her eyes. "Fine, but then I'll buy you mulled wine!"

"Sounds good to me," Jonas replied, tucking the music box in with the other presents. Before he had finished, Sophie had already hopped over to the mulled wine stall. Although she was wearing a thick coat and lined boots, Jonas could see her prancing and balancing on her toes. The music was always in her, and he wished, not for the first time, that he could share it with her. It might banish the eternal thoughts of war in him.

A little later, they were leaning against the wall of a hut with their two steaming mugs of mulled wine, enjoying the spicy aroma.

"You know, Jonas, I've been thinking," she suddenly began, atypically serious. "The curse will be broken in May, and even though at the moment, I would like nothing more than to sleep through the better part of three months, I think I'd like to go back to ballet."

Astonished, Jonas turned to her. "Really? I thought you hated it since...?"

Sophie looked bashful. "I guess the lie was never that convincing."

He thought back to the days when she'd found time to work out in her little studio. How she'd spent hours dancing through her old routines and how wonderful she'd looked doing it. It was a load off Jonas' mind that she was now willing to give it another try. She loved ballet, always had.

"It's going to be hard to get back into shape, of course, but at least I'm fit thanks to Luca," Sophie continued. "I've even had a look around. They're having auditions at the ballet school for the next year's class in January, so I thought I might try out for that."

"Not maybe," Jonas objected. "Do it. The class doesn't start until summer?" Sophie nodded slightly. "Then, by all means. You don't want to lose another year. I think you should get back to ballet as soon as possible."

Sophie frowned. "Why?"

"Because you love it," Jonas explained with a passion he couldn't muster for anything else. "And because you come alive when you dance. You're good, incredibly good. In my opinion, you could dance on the biggest stages in the world."

Sophie smiled warmly at him, then nestled her head against his shoulder. "You really mean that, don't you?"

Jonas nodded. "Definitely."

"Thank you."

They enjoyed the moment in silence, drinking their mulled wine. The sky had become darker, and now large white flakes were falling from the sky. The first ones were melting on the cobblestones, but more flakes were swirling through the air, covering streets and houses with glorious white.

Cheering, Sophie pushed her empty cup into Jonas' hand and spun in circles like the little ballerina in her music box. The snowflakes caught in her blonde hair and he became completely lost in the enchanting sight.

Her childlike joy at the snow finally put him in the Christmas spirit. When she held out her hand to him, Jonas grinned and let himself be pulled along by her. Together, they spun in a circle. Sophie's eyes sparkled with joy as her cheeks reddened in the cold. Her hands, holding him close, were cold in his.

Sophie's joy filled him from head to toe and warmed him more than the mulled wine had. At that moment, he fell in love with her all over again. He loved her sparkling eyes. The little dimples. The snow in her hair. But most of all, her laugh.

―

Christmas lunch at Sophie's father's was a strange affair. The hall—it could hardly be called anything else—was far too big for the three of them and the waiter created a ghastly formal atmosphere. If it weren't for Sophie, who sat opposite him, smirking now and then, Jonas would've felt like he was at a business dinner.

If he missed a behavioural cue or was about to talk his head off, she would nudge him with her foot. Each time it happened, the touch ran through him like an electric shock, and Jonas found it difficult to follow Mr Kallenbach.

Sophie was hyper from the five cups of coffee she had downed in the morning so she could get through the day. The entire time she was sliding around in her chair, almost bubbling over with excitement. Before they'd left, she'd even coerced Jonas into opening his present, even though they'd agreed to do it for the afternoon.

It had been a book about architecture, and as he leafed through the glossy pages, the old desire had come back to the surface. His head had immediately filled with ideas, so much so he would have preferred to stay at home and put them on paper. Instead, he was suffering through this surreal Christmas lunch.

"By the way, Jonas has a few audition dates lined up for me," Sophie told her father all at once, and Jonas sensed that she was teasing the old man. He knew by now that Mr Kallenbach was not well disposed towards his daughter's dancing ambitions. "They're looking for some dancers to join their company at the old theatre."

While his enthusiasm was indeed limited, her father made an effort. "Is that so? Does that mean you want to go professional?"

"Why not? Jonas thinks I'd be very good," Sophie replied, looking at him in a teasing way. "Isn't that right?"

Jonas felt a flush of red settle on his cheeks that was definitely not from the wine. He could hardly take his eyes off Sophie's beautiful face to confirm her words. "Excellent, yes. You'd think she was a prima ballerina already."

Her father sighed. "Well, I can't say I'm particularly surprised by this, and I know that you're talented enough. Just... are you sure? Dancing?" There was a lot of pain in his words, and the thought of Sophie's mother sobered Jonas a little.

"What's wrong with dancing?" asked Sophie provocatively.

Mr Kallenbach gave her a long look that made Jonas want to sink into his chair. Not so Sophie, who smiled sweetly at her father as if she couldn't hurt a fly. "Well, for example, what profession do you want to take up when your stage days are over? Have you thought about that, too?"

Groaning, Sophie leaned back and rolled her eyes. "Here I am, finally making a decision about my future, and you want me to think even further ahead! I can't have my whole life planned out, can I?" Then she turned her flighty attention back to Jonas and chewed on her lower lip.

Although Jonas had been drinking a moment ago, his throat suddenly went dry.

"It's fine," her father relented. "And who's funding this?"

Laughing, Sophie looked at him again. "Dad, if I have an engagement at the theatre, I'll earn money, and who knows, maybe I'll take up pole-dancing after all."

Mr Kallenbach sighed, turning his attention on Jonas instead. "And what about you? Can I still count on you in the new year, or do you have other plans?"

Overwhelmed by Sophie's overflowing energy and Mr Kallenbach's stern look, Jonas found himself at a loss for words. "Uh, I..."

"Of course Jonas is staying. He's part of the family now," Sophie interrupted him in a surprise move, causing a pleasant tugging in his stomach. "Someone has to support me on my rocky road to becoming a prima ballerina if you don't."

The look her father gave Jonas was frighteningly helpless. Mr Kallenbach seemed just as overwhelmed by Sophie's outrageous behaviour as Jonas was.

"I want to stay in town for now, yes," Jonas confirmed. "I like the job." More than that, it was the routine and financial security the job offered him that he loved. And that Mr Kallenbach didn't take offence when he struggled with his visions once in a while.

"Good," Sophie's father agreed, even smiling at Jonas. "I didn't mean to imply that I was unhappy with your work, either. Quite the opposite. I was thinking of employing you in a different position to further your career. Maybe even abroad."

The prospect gave Jonas a stomachache. With Sophie, he had found a safe haven. Even if he lost his job, eventually, because the nightmares were getting worse with each passing day, she had promised that he could stay with her. If he left now, he knew he would lose it completely.

The terror must have been written all over his face, for Sophie suddenly glared at her father. "Dad, I meant what I said. I need Jonas. He's helping me with the audition, isn't he?

Without him, I would never have had the courage to sign up for it last week."

In fact, she had raised all possible and impossible counter-arguments before Jonas had been able to persuade her to send in the application. That she hadn't discussed it with Luca yet, even though she had had time to do so every night. That she didn't have time to prepare now, although she could easily use her late-night dancing for that occasion. And that the date was too inconvenient for her. After all, she would have to be back at The DeModie only two and a half hours after the start of the auditions.

He had refuted all excuses and given her a good talking to. In the end, Jonas had even managed to rouse her enthusiasm, and from that point on, it was Sophie's excitement that had carried them both away. "It matters to him that I go through with it, and I have to admit that his support is immensely motivating. For the first time since Mum died, I think I really could do this."

Sophie's words made the room temperature drop what felt like ten degrees, and Jonas held his breath.

Her father's features were transfixed, and his voice was entirely flat when he said, "I see. Well then, I suppose I have to thank you, Jonas."

"Don't mention it," Jonas hastened to say. He was terribly uncomfortable with the whole affair. "As I said, I really think if anyone can do it, it's Sophie." Cautiously, he smiled at her. "We'll get you back on stage."

Her warm smile was answer enough for him.

On New Year's Eve, the visions got worse. All day Jonas had been terribly tense, while his hands had started shaking again. The alcohol in his blood numbed the worst of it, but every premature bang startled him.

As Sophie began to dress for the New Year's Eve party at The DeModie, he almost begged her to stay with him. With her, he would make it through the night. Her laughter kept him in this reality. But he knew her answer, even without having to ask. He would have to put on his big boy pants for this.

The darkness brought more terrors. They lurked in the shadows of every room, following Jonas at every turn and startling him. In response, he switched on every single light in the house and checked all the corners. Then he settled down in front of the TV with a bottle of beer and zapped wildly through the channels.

Countdowns were displayed everywhere and inevitably attracted his gaze. It was the time he had left before disaster struck. There was nothing left of the peaceful Christmas atmosphere. Now everyone was out to celebrate wildly and loudly. Annoyed, Jonas switched the TV off again to escape the miserable clocks.

Restless, Jonas strode through all the rooms once more, checking possible hiding places. He knew he was in Sophie's flat and that no one would be able to harm him here. And yet, the waiting began to drive him crazy. It only stopped when he entered the dance studio.

In the mirror, he saw Sophie jumping high and arching her back. She lifted her free leg above her head and pirouetted endlessly on the spot. Every fibre of her body was stretched and moved in unison with the music. He could almost hear the melody.

Determined, he strode across the room and switched on the stereo. The sounds of *Giselle* drowned out the scattered rockets outside, but they weren't enough to relieve Jonas' tension. He had to do something before he started pacing around the room again, driving himself crazy. Finally, he got his pad from his room and began to capture the images of Sophie from his mind on paper.

Jonas knew exactly at which point in the music she jumped and where she paused. He remembered her rehearsals as clear as day. The way her body twisted and stretched was so familiar to him that he effortlessly put her form on paper. At some point, he moved on to emphasising the facial features he knew by heart, and the drawings of her figures became portraits that sought to capture her radiant laughter. Picture after picture Jonas drew, so completely absorbed in his memories that he didn't notice how time passed.

Until the clock struck twelve.

All at once, the previously isolated rockets multiplied by a hundred and ignited straight above him. Jonas threw himself to the ground and threw his hands over his head as he frantically searched for cover. But everywhere he looked, there were faces.

His own eyes didn't stare back at him from the mirrors, but the bloody faces of his comrades and injured civilians. Between them, the Taliban stood, looking for him and his squad, while more grenades exploded around them.

Paralysed, Jonas crouched on the spot, not knowing where to flee to. They would get him this time. He wouldn't have outrageous luck again.

Pain shot through his shoulder, and for a moment, he rolled on the floor screaming until the fear of being discovered took over again. Other screams rang out around him. Terrible cries of pain and fear. Screams he would never forget. And in between, the crying of a child standing abandoned in the middle of the street, reaching out to him.

Jonas wanted to help so much—that was what he had come here for after all—but he couldn't. Try as he might, he couldn't get his legs to stand up, didn't dare give up what little cover he had. He was trapped in this hell until they were all dead or the Taliban moved on.

But he had to live. He couldn't die here. Back in Germany, his parents were waiting for him to come home. If only he would have. He was a coward, a giant coward. Because he couldn't even get up and save the child. Because he couldn't even help Philipp, who was rolling on the ground in agony not three metres away from him. Because he couldn't even admit to himself that he needed help. A lot of it.

All Jonas could do was huddle on the floor and remain there, hoping against the odds he'd survive one more night. Glass splintered around him and covered him like a blanket. The sharp edges stung the back of his neck. *Don't move now. That's what they were waiting for.*

Where was his helmet? The thought appeared suddenly in his mind and pushed everything else aside. He needed his helmet, otherwise he was doomed to die with the next explosion. Panic-stricken, Jonas crawled across the floor and searched blindly for the lost piece of armour. Philipp had died because he hadn't had his helmet on. His blood was still on Jonas' trembling hands.

Suddenly, there was someone else. Two heavy boots stepped up beside him until they were right in front of his face. Shuddering miserably, Jonas looked up. They had found him, he thought, as the barrel of a gun aimed at him. In a moment, it would be over.

No! He didn't want to die. Not like this. Not 5,000 kilometres from home. He found the strength to leap up and rammed his head into the pit of the enemy's stomach. They both went down under Jonas' weight and hit the hard, dusty earth. Before his enemy could react, Jonas slammed his forearm into their throat and pressed down. If he'd had a weapon at hand, he would have used it, but as it was, he was left with instinct and brute strength alone.

Fingers clawed at his forearm in a desperate attempt to take the pressure off their throat and Jonas could hear the strained gasp of air rushing in his ears. Then the slender fingers reached for his face, slapping him weakly and scratching his face.

Blood ran down Jonas' chin, and the scratch on his cheek burned like hell. The pain was so much stronger and more vivid than anything else around him.

The scratch was real; he realised all at once and shuddered violently when he recognised Sophie. Tears of despair streamed down her face. She gasped for breath as her fingers searched more feebly than ever for his face.

On the spot, Jonas let go of her, got to his feet, and stumbled until his back hit the barre on the opposite wall. Trembling, he lowered himself against the mirror and stared wide-eyed at Sophie, who rolled onto all fours, coughing and gasping.

Sunlight broke in the mirrors and lit up the whole room. He was home, the war long behind him. But as Sophie had said, his head was still in Afghanistan. He was too weak, too weak to shake off the memories, and now he had almost killed Sophie.

"I'm so sorry," he croaked, feeling the tears coming. "I'm so terribly sorry."

Sophie looked at him, her dark eyes still dilated with terror. The colour slowly returned to her face, however, and her breathing calmed.

Instead, the lump in Jonas' throat threatened to cut off his breath now. "I didn't mean to. I didn't know it was you. I didn't even realise it was morning," he tried to explain, cursing himself for his pathetic babbling. "I'm so sorry."

Slowly, the fear disappeared from Sophie's face, and she came to sit on her knees. "What happened?"

Ashamed, Jonas lowered his eyes. "I was back in the war. You were right," he admitted in an increasingly shaky voice. "I'm still there and always will be. It was hell." Instead of facing her, he looked down at his hands, which were shaking so badly he wanted to sit on them. The shadow of a cloud passed by the window, and all at once, the blood of days long past shimmered on the palms of his hands, threatening to pull him straight back.

"I see it all, all the time. The ruined houses. The smoke. The dead." Jonas swallowed. "I can't escape them. The Taliban are looking for me. Want revenge for us being there. Yet, we only want to help. We're not an assault team at all." He couldn't say any more. The pressure in his head was too great. His throat hurt more with every second.

Suddenly, he felt her fingers gently brush against his chin and then across his cheeks. "Oh, Jonas."

For a moment, he allowed the touch, eager to put the attack behind him and forget about it in Sophie's presence. But then Jonas saw the bruising under her chin, and he knew what he had to do.

Confused, Sophie stared at him as he suddenly rose and walked purposefully towards the door. "What are you up to?" she called after him, getting to her feet as well.

Only with difficulty did Jonas manage to control his voice. "I've hurt you. That's unforgivable. Which means I need to leave." He glared back. "I'm a danger to you." It was a mistake to look back. Sophie had her arms wrapped protectively around her body. There was an unspoken plea in her eyes. "You need to understand, Sophie. I can't stay."

"And where will you go?" Before he could answer, Sophie spoke on, her voice strangely strained, "You'll have no money, no roof over your head, and no job if you leave now."

"I have a bit saved up. I'll find something. Don't worry about me!"

Defiantly, Sophie shook her head. "This is ridiculous, Jonas. You were having a fit. You didn't mean to hurt me. I'm sure it was because of the firecrackers, but you'll be at peace from them for a year, and next time, I'll be with you. You can't leave me alone now."

Jonas sighed. He wanted to stay, but in view of what he had experienced, it was impossible. "You're not alone. You still have Luca and your father. They won't try to strangle you."

"I'm not afraid of you." Her own eyes belied her words, or perhaps it was guilt that made him think so. "I told you that you could stay here until you were better. Right now, you're far from well, so please stay!"

"This isn't about me," Jonas objected, pained. "I don't want you to have to wonder if it's safe to come home today. Or if I've torn your flat apart again. Or..."

"But it's not your fault," Sophie interrupted him. "You've been through hell. It's only understandable that you can't just brush that aside." Her words sounded so logical, so harmless. As if he hadn't just attempted to take her life.

His stomach clenched at the thought of what would have happened if he hadn't snapped out of it in time. "Sophie..."

"I need you, Jonas," she said once more. She had said something along those lines already to her father.

Jonas tried to ignore the warm feeling that was spreading inside him. He didn't deserve this. Not now. Not ever.

"You're the only one who believes in me."

His mouth went dry, but still he forced out the words that needed to be said. "What about Luca?"

Nervously, Sophie snorted. "Nothing. Well... He doesn't support me like you do. I mean how could he when he's tied to the club? For him... Other things matter to us right now. But you..." She bit her lip, and Jonas felt his resolve begin to soften. "You care about me. My happiness and health matters to you, and I'm sure I wouldn't have begun to dream of dancing again without your annoying prodding."

A tentative smile spread across Jonas' face. "Thanks for saying that." Still, he couldn't give in. For her sake. "But you can do it without me. You were born to dance, and you don't need me for that. I don't even know anything about ballet. I'm just..." Annoyed by his own ramblings, Jonas tensed. "It's not worth the risk."

"Dance with me!" Sophie urged him all of the sudden, holding out her hands. Confused by her sudden change of subject, Jonas could only stare at her. Sophie smiled nervously. "Come on, Jonas. Give me your hands!"

"Why? What..."

"Don't ask! Come here!" Hesitantly, Jonas stepped closer until Sophie took hold of his hands. "Music always helps me when my thoughts are spinning, and I don't know what to do with my feelings." Without looking him in the face, she placed his left hand on the small of her back and placed hers on his shoulder.

"I can't dance," Jonas warned, still doubtful this would solve any of his problems. Or lessen the danger to Sophie.

Sophie wasn't fazed by this. "Just follow the music!"

"What music?" he asked, irritated. The stereo had gone silent hours ago.

Embarrassed, Sophie broke away from him once more. "Oh yes. You can't actually hear the music in my head."

As she walked to the stereo, he was tempted to flee. It would have been better for the both of them.

"I can't get it out of my head," Sophie said, finally choosing a CD.

The first notes sounded delicate and soft in the air as they resumed their positions. "Lower your hand a little," Sophie instructed him, and the lump in his throat appeared again. "Can you hear the music now?"

Jonas nodded and was rewarded by Sophie's radiant smile. Gently, she guided him, not bothering with big jumps or complex figures. Instead, she was simply close to him, snuggling up to his chest, swaying to the beat. If his steps were still stiff at the beginning, Sophie's closeness made him loosen up.

Slowly, the memories that held him captive subsided, and with each gentle movement, the terror faded. As the music filled his mind and body, a cautious thought crept in. Perhaps he could stay after all. Stay just a little longer in Sophie's arms, while bright spots of the New Year's sun danced across the floor.

Dégagè

Sophie had been standing outside her front door for twenty minutes, contemplating the doorknob. Only a tiny turn stood between her and her long-awaited bed. Only the door and Jonas.

She could hear him inside. Although it was still early in the morning, he was already on his feet. Dishes clanked, drawers rattled, and footsteps echoed across the parquet floor. She had hoped he'd still be asleep, although he hardly ever was when she came home. He always seemed to be waiting for her. Like her mother used to do when Sophie had overstayed her curfew.

Although she fought it with all her might, she couldn't banish the images of New Year's Day from her mind. The fear in Jonas' eyes. The despair as he squeezed her throat shut. The pain in her lungs. Even the memory of it made it hard to breathe.

Sweat trickled down her back, and all at once, Sophie felt so dizzy she had to sit down on the steps. Surely it was only the lack of sleep and not fear of Jonas. Jonas, who always cared about her, whose beacon of light she was — which he never tired of emphasising — and who always looked at her so longingly. He would never knowingly hurt her.

And yet he had.

Although Sophie had witnessed the odd fit, she'd never cared. He'd spoken of the nightmares, but she'd been dancing every night, and when she slept during the day, it was so sound that not even one of Jonas' grenades could have woken her. It was entirely possible that the visions haunted him considerably more often than she'd suspected, that at this very moment another had taken control, making him unable to distinguish between memory and reality.

Her whole body trembled at the idea. Suddenly, she heard footsteps behind the door. Sophie had just enough time to jump back up and brush a strand of hair from her face before the door opened.

Jonas looked at her in confusion. "Sophie. Did you forget your key?"

"Key?" It took a moment for the meaning to sink in. "Not exactly. It's in my handbag, but there's so much stuff in there..."

To her surprise, Jonas smiled. "Well, then you're lucky I'm still here. I was just about to leave."

"So early? Is my father even awake?" asked Sophie, interlacing her fingers so they stopped shaking.

"I don't know, but I'm sure yesterday's orders are still on his desk. Breakfast is on the table for you." He glanced behind for a moment, and Sophie followed his gaze.

In fact, the dining table was almost spilling over with food. Fresh rolls, various cold cuts, a boiled egg. There was even a fruit plate. To top it all off, he had provided flowers. Sophie swallowed. Everything about it screamed apology. "Is that for me?"

"Well, it's certainly not for the postman," Jonas commented dryly. "Have a seat and eat. I'll be back at three to pick you up."

The whole affair was becoming more and more confusing. "Why?"

There was an amused twinkle in his eyes that seemed entirely unnatural in his face. "Because we're going into town to get you some new pointe shoes. You can't very well turn up at the audition in those rags."

Startled, Sophie gasped, but Jonas was right. The shoes on her feet deserved the label. No one would take her seriously at the audition if she wore these. Still, she was too tired to feel any enthusiasm at the prospect of visiting the dance shop. "Alright, if you say so."

"I do." Jonas smiled at her one last time, then he grabbed his backpack next to the door. "Get a good rest."

Uncertain, Sophie watched him go until he'd disappeared into the main house. If she didn't know better, she would have believed the nightmares no longer bothered him.

Sighing, she finally entered her house and closed the door behind her. The smell of fresh bread rolls didn't trigger any appetite in her, and even the fruit plate left her completely cold. All she wanted was to slip into her warm bed and sleep for half a year.

❧

"What do I need new shoes for, anyway? My feet are already used to the old ones," Sophie whined as the shop assistant disappeared into the storeroom for a second time. "Besides, the others bring me luck." She was still too tired, and the shop reminded her far too much of her youth. Any moment now, she expected her mother to round the corner with a new box.

But she didn't.

Crossing his arms in front of his chest, Jonas sceptically raised an eyebrow. "Oh, yeah?"

Her cheeks burned with anger, and she had to bite her tongue to keep from snapping at him. To make matters worse, she couldn't even think of a good example to dispel his doubts. Just the one, "They led me to Luca."

"Right." Now, Jonas was studying the carpet. Luca was always a tender subject between them. But then he added, "You're the expert. If you say the people at the audition won't pay attention to sensible footwear and you're confident you can dance your routine with broken shoes, that's what you've got to do." Almost casually, he added, "Didn't you just complain at Christmas that the pointe was ruined?"

Sophie could only throw him an acid stare since the shop-keeper returned with a new stack of boxes then. "Try these and see if they're hard enough for your taste." The woman recommended a pair.

Sighing, Sophie accepted and turned around. She was embarrassed to bare her feet in front of her. Sore feet were not uncommon among ballet dancers. But hers had just been pushed a little beyond the limit. If she wanted reproachful looks, she only had to ask Jonas.

Fortunately, he noticed her discomfort. "Do you have them in other colours?" he inquired. The woman raised both eyebrows at him.

Sophie bit her tongue. Jonas had no way of knowing that flashy colours weren't welcome at an audition. The saleswoman gave Sophie another long look before shaking her head and leaving the room.

Silently, Sophie slipped into the shoes and tied them. The lady had been right. They met her requirements exactly and fit well. The fact that the fabric pinched in some places was due more to the condition of her feet than the pretty shoes. She actually liked them the longer she looked at them. They almost made her feel like a real ballerina again.

With a tingle, anticipation gripped her. She would actually return to the stage, maybe even make it into the company. From a young age, her dream had always been to be a prima ballerina, just as her mother had been. If only her feet didn't hurt so much all the time. *Grit your teeth and get up*, she heard in her inner ear. That was how it had always been in ballet.

Sophie wiped away all misgivings and immediately stood on pointe. Pain shot through her from toe to calf. Only through years of training did she manage to maintain her posture and slowly return to first position.

"Are you all right?" Startled, Sophie winced and fell back onto the stool. She had forgotten all about Jonas. "That looked painful." Obviously, she had been far less in control of her face than her posture.

Concerned, Jonas knelt in front of her and slowly removed the shoes from her feet. "It's alright. It..." She broke off as he silently looked at the sore spots.

Sophie's throat tightened. "Ballerina feet aren't pretty," she tried to explain, blinking against the sudden tears in her eyes.

"It gets worse every day," Jonas remarked thoughtfully. When he looked up at her, she could hardly bear his pity. "What do you think about wearing more comfortable shoes for The DeModie? Sneakers or something?"

"No!" Her vehemence surprised even Sophie. For a moment, the thought had sent an icy chill down her spine.

Jonas stared at her, and she knew she had to say something. "Ballet shoes need to be broken in, and I only have a few weeks left until the audition."

"Okay." His reply sounded strangely toneless, but at least he'd accepted her excuse.

The mood between them was subdued when they left the shop with the new shoes. Jonas seemed to have his mind elsewhere and Sophie didn't know how to return to the relaxed atmosphere she had destroyed with her snotty answers. They walked side by side in silence until they were almost home.

"Are you going to eat something before you go?" asked Jonas.

A glance at the clock answered the question. "No, I'll get something once I'm there." She had never asked before, but Tomas would know how to conjure up some food. After all, Luca, his brothers, and all the others had to eat something, too.

While she picked a dress and disappeared into the bathroom for half an hour, Jonas put away the breakfast dishes and started washing up. The sight had become a habit for Sophie, and a smile stole onto her lips.

"When the days get longer, we'll eat together again, I promise." She reached for her dancing shoes.

Snorting, Jonas replied, his back turned to her, "I'd be happy just knowing you're eating anything at all."

Sophie rolled her eyes. "I'm eating. Don't worry."

"You'll need your strength," Jonas said, turning around. "What are you doing?"

Confused, Sophie looked from the shoes she had slipped on to him and back again. Without realising it, she had put on the old ones. She briefly considered taking them off, but they felt too good for that. Not as hard and unyielding as the new ones that put pressure on every sore spot. These shoes had the same quirks as she did. They belonged to her.

Determined, Sophie straightened up. "I can't get through a night in the new ones yet. I'll do that another time." She ignored the disappointment in his gaze as best she could.

"Okay." That toneless voice again. "But remember, you wanted to practise your routine."

"Yes, Dad." The words slipped out before she could control herself. Fortunately, Jonas didn't hold it against her, instead smiling faintly at her. A little more conciliatory, Sophie took her leave. "See you in the morning."

"Good evening, Tomas." Sophie greeted the young bouncer and gave him a brief hug. "I really need something to drink before I pass out."

Laughing, Tomas closed the door behind them. "Coming right up, Princess Sophie."

Smirking, she allowed her coat to be removed. It was a little quirk of Tomas' that he had been calling her a princess for months. "It's cold outside, let me tell you. It's been snowing again. My feet are probably lumps of ice by now." Unbidden, the thought of Jonas' disapproval regarding her choice of shoes came to mind.

Tomas just grinned and led her down the stairs. "I'm sure Luca will warm them up for you quickly."

For a moment, Sophie tried to imagine Luca bringing her warm water or rubbing her feet between his hands. It didn't work. That was Jonas' way, not Lucas'. As a prince, he'd always had servants for that sort of thing.

"Say, you wouldn't happen to have anything on offer for dinner? I didn't manage to get anything to eat beforehand."

Yawning, Sophie put a hand over her mouth. Even though she'd only been awake for three hours, she would have liked to climb straight back into bed. "These long nights are really exhausting and I feel like I can't get anything else done."

Pityingly, Tomas patted her on the shoulder. "Let's have a drink first and then we'll see about the rest."

He disappeared from her side as soon as they reached the bottom of the stairs. Luca was already waiting. He gallantly extended his hand to her. "Welcome back, beautiful."

Giggling, Sophie placed her hand in his and let him greet her with a kiss. The sun must have barely set before the first sounds of music could be heard. Her feet were already tingling in anticipation, while the rest of her body longed for a break still.

Then Tomas reappeared at her side and handed her his special blue drink. "Here you go, extra strong for you." Turning to Luca, he explained, "Sophie is tired."

Even as he said it, she felt the tiredness drain from her body with each successive sip.

Luca merely nodded and regarded Sophie questioningly. "Shall we dance?"

She stared at him in puzzlement. It was as if he hadn't even heard Tomas. "Uh... yeah, sure." She handed the half empty glass back to the younger brother and took Luca's other hand. "Let's go for it."

His radiant smile compensated her instantly. In fact, Sophie was much more comfortable with him not stalking her with worry, like Jonas. After all, she came to The DeModie to have a good time.

Together, they entered the dance floor, which was still quite empty at this hour. Not that it bothered Sophie. The wondrous cocktail warmed her from the inside and filled her with new life. Her feet were already moving, almost by themselves, to the beat of the music. She didn't need anything more than the presence of her handsome prince.

"You know what, Luca? I was thinking of taking up ballet again. After I free you, I mean," Sophie told him as he swung her around. "I've had a bit of a break, but I'm sure I'll get back into it quickly. I even booked an audition. The week after next. You can't imagine how excited I am."

Her dancing had attracted the other residents of The De-Modie, and Sophie shivered in anticipation. Soon, they'd be coming for her. Her unease must've got through to Luca, because he shooed the pitiful figures away. Then he pulled Sophie to him and murmured in a low voice, "Tonight you belong only to me."

A comforting shiver ran down her spine as his lips settled on hers. His mouth was as sweet as the cocktail, and Sophie couldn't get enough of his kisses. All too soon, Luca broke away from her and returned to the dance and to their conversation. "An audition, yes?"

"Yes, it's with the company down at the City Theatre. If I get accepted, it would be amazing." It was the same company her mother had once danced with. If only she were still able to see her dancing there.

Luca didn't sound too enthusiastic when he said, "That sounds pretty exhausting. Maybe that's why you're so tired. Why don't you just wait a little longer, Sophie? It's not like the company is getting away from you."

Disappointed, she protested, "But I want to do this. I can't just sleep all day."

"But you're dancing at night," Luca countered.

"I promised my father, and besides..." Angrily, Sophie blinked against the sudden pressure in her eyes. "Why would it be such a bad idea to attempt this now?"

Luca stroked her cheek. "I'm afraid you're taking on too much. I can see how exhausting breaking my curse is for you."

So, he *did* care!

A pleasant warmth spread through her, and she quickly stole another kiss before he twirled her across the lake again. "I promise to take care of myself. Besides, I can combine pleasure and work, can't I? I'll be at The DeModie all night. I might as well practise my choreography here. I brought some of my music. Do you think Bastien could put it on?"

"No."

As if struck by lightning, Sophie stopped and stared at Luca. He immediately took her in his arms and sighed. "Darling, you know that's not possible. There's only the one music in The DeModie. And besides, I'm sure your choreography doesn't require a partner. Or is there one waiting for you outside?"

For a moment, she saw jealousy flash in his eyes and had to think of Jonas. She'd never told Luca about him.

When she shook her head, Luca put his fingers under her chin and smiled at her. "The curse requires us to dance with each other, not beside each other. Under different circumstances, I would love to watch your ballet."

Sophie couldn't deny the importance of his words, but the expected relief failed to materialise.

"You'll see," Luca said. "Once the year is over, we'll go for it together. That would be something, wouldn't it? You and me, in the same company, on stage together."

She liked the idea. With a smile, she let herself be kissed again and finally nodded. "That sounds exceptional." She would find another way to make Jonas and her father happy.

⁓

An obnoxious beep interrupted the melody of her dream and jolted Sophie from her sleep. Overtired, she groped for her bedside table and switched off the alarm clock that had woken her for training. It felt like she had just gone to bed. Frustrated, she realised it was already three o'clock. Her head throbbed incessantly, the light blinded her, and there was a static in her ears.

Sophie buried herself deeper into the blankets and closed her eyes. Only a moment later—or so it felt—she heard the key in the door and Jonas' footsteps in the hallway. Shortly after, there was a knock against her bedroom door. "Are you awake, Sophie?"

For a moment, she considered pretending to be asleep, but then she dismissed the thought and flipped back the covers. "I'll be up in a minute."

"Alright." The footsteps moved away again.

Sophie climbed out of bed and got dressed, yawning incessantly. Now that it was time for it, she had little desire to start training. But if she didn't, her father would surely come down on her again. Besides, Jonas was so obsessed with helping her with her new venture that she couldn't possibly give up before she'd even started.

A little later, Sophie finally entered the small studio and started warming up. Jonas sat in a corner as before, his drawing pad on his lap. His gaze, however, flitted back and forth, and instead of drawing, he merely tapped the pencil on the paper.

"Would you rather go into the living room?" asked Sophie. After all, it had only been four days since he'd seen the ghosts of his past here.

Jonas looked up and shook his head. "I'm not going to pass up the chance to see you dance again."

His confession only elicited a weary smile from her. She stifled a yawn and selected her piece. In position, she awaited the first notes and was irritated when they sounded quite different from what she'd expected. It was the correct song, but the static in her ears distorted the sound, and her feet couldn't find the right rhythm. She was always half a second late until, at last, she stumbled out of time altogether.

With long strides, Sophie reached the stereo and pressed stop. The music faded away and made way for the melody of her nights. Her pulse raced and incomprehension rolled through her insides like an avalanche. She hadn't danced as badly as she had just now for a very long time. As if she didn't have the slightest sense of time.

"Try again!" Jonas said.

Sophie realised how stupid she must look right now: her hands clenched into fists as if she was about to hit the stereo. And yet, the technology was least to blame for her sudden inability.

Jonas stood up and walked over. His hand fell on her shoulder, and for a tiny moment, Sophie tensed. "Don't be so hard on yourself! You haven't done any ballet for months now. You probably need to ease your way back in."

"I know how to dance," Sophie replied defiantly, but the uncertainty gnawed at her. It had been two years since she'd last been to a proper class. And five months since she'd given up repetitions in her small studio for Luca. When she went dancing at The DeModie, she danced all sorts of styles, but not the clean-cut lines that ballet demanded of her.

"I know that," Jonas reassured her, rubbing her shoulder in comfort. When he took his hand away again, Sophie sighed in relief. It wasn't that she hadn't enjoyed his touch, but it reminded her too much of the last time she had spoken to him in here. "You need to give yourself some time. It'll come with practise. How was it last night?"

Confused, Sophie looked at him. "What do you mean?"

"Well, did it go better at The DeModie?"

No, I wasn't allowed to practise there. The answer raced through her mind. But if she told him that, he'd have another fit. "A little. But I wasn't completely overtired then either."

"You just got up," he remarked, frowning. Before she could say anything back, Jonas had stepped forward and clicked play on her chosen piece. "Come on, you can do it. You just have to keep at it."

He was right. She had to keep trying. It wasn't like she'd always nailed her choreography on the first try in the past. On the other hand, she had never fumbled as badly as she had just now. Once again, the music struggled to penetrate Sophie's befuddled mind, and she kept missing her cues. At The DeModie, her feet seemed to dance by themselves. Now they ached with every step and wouldn't let her give it her best.

The harder she tried, the worse it got. The music seemed strange and unpleasant. She didn't even know why she had chosen this piece in the first place. It sounded just awful.

Sophie stomped her feet in frustration and then dropped to the floor. Wrapping her arms around her legs, she rested her head on her knees and tried to ignore the burning in her eyes. But she couldn't stop the tears.

Jonas relented on her and turned off the stereo. "Maybe it's just not working today."

"It's never going to work again," she said.

"You know that's nonsense, Sophie." He took a seat opposite her. "You can do it. You're just a little out of practice, that's all. But we'll get it right. You'll see, in a few days you'll be laughing about it. There are still two weeks, Sophie. If we practise every day..."

"I'm tired." She interrupted his motivational speech and glared at him. She wanted to say something witty, but the arguments eluded her as much as the choreography.

Jonas regarded her with pity. Carefully, he put an arm around her shoulders, and this time, Sophie welcomed his closeness. It felt good to know she wasn't struggling alone.

After a while, Jonas whispered softly, "Tell me how I can help you. I... You know I would do anything for you."

"There's nothing you can do. It's all up to me," Sophie objected, sighing heavily. "I just need a drink."

Puzzled, Jonas looked at her and straightened up a little. "A drink? You mean some water or coffee? I can put some on." With regret, she noticed him pull his arm back.

Sophie shook her head and sat up straight as well. "No, I mean the cocktail Tomas makes me. One of those special mixes. Once I drink it, I'm like a changed person. My feet don't hurt, I don't have to yawn all the time, and—"

With every word, Jonas's gaze had become darker, and slowly Sophie fell silent. Her throat felt dry, and the fear returned. But he didn't lapse into another vision of terror. Instead, he grumbled in a bad temper, "Drugs? Luca is having you drugged?"

"No!" The absurdity of this thought frightened Sophie. "I would never take anything like that. It's a totally harmless drink, like coffee. It's probably got guarana in it."

Jonas' stare seemed to pierce her. "But it doesn't sound like coffee. Sophie, if they give you shit like that there—"

"It's not drugs!" Groaning, Sophie ran her hands over her face. "You've got to believe me!"

"Drugs and lots of alcohol," Jonas muttered before sighing at last. "I believe you, but I don't trust Luca, or Tomas for that matter. That guy—"

When he went down that route again, Sophie couldn't take it any longer. She jumped up and reached for the towel. "You know what? I have to go now. We'll practise more tomorrow. I'll try my best, too. I promise."

"Sophie..." The desperation in his voice almost caused her to burst into tears her nerves had become that thin.

Hastily, she turned away. "I'll see you later." She fled the room before Jonas had even got to his feet.

~

The nights at The DeModie were getting wilder by the day. Soon, Sophie couldn't tell reality from her dreams. When she swept across the dance floor with Luca, horrible creatures crowded around her, touching her and feasting on her life force. Sometimes it hurt, but Luca's affection quickly made her forget the pain.

She was entirely convinced that no one would dare to seriously harm her in his presence. And Luca was always there. He held her in his arms and guided her impeccably, despite the tight space. Whenever she was tired, he would wave to Tomas, and a little later she'd refuel with one of his infamous blue cocktails.

In the process, they hardly retreated into their boat. Sophie was fine with that. When she was at The DeModie, she wanted to dance, not talk. What was she even supposed to talk about with Luca? They had known each other for so long, and until the curse was defeated, she didn't need to talk about her plans for the future either. She hadn't told him that she still wanted to go to the audition. After all, he had made it abundantly clear that he didn't think it was a good idea. She needed her energy for The DeModie. For him.

By now, Sophie was convinced that Luca was right. The practice sessions with Jonas were draining her, and he was also becoming more irritable by the day. Far too often, she saw him staring into emptiness, blind to reality. Whenever he approached her, however, he had himself under control, and slowly, she'd begun to trust him again.

Sophie would have loved to help him, but she didn't have the strength. She hardly saw him in the morning, and in the afternoon, they worked hard for the audition. She had painstakingly learned the choreography, although it was still difficult for her. Her cues worked and her technique was flawless, but she couldn't manage to sink into the music.

In The DeModie, the notes filled her every nerve. There was not a single song where she didn't feel a deep connection. In contrast, the dancing at home was devoid of any feeling, almost lifeless. Jonas kept trying to build her up, but Sophie just couldn't get over it. She was convinced she wouldn't even get to the next round at the audition.

"Ow!" A sharp pain went through her upper left arm. Someone had bitten her.

Fascinated, Sophie observed the drops of blood that spilled from her arm in time to the beat. The melody washed away the pain, and while Luca was still confronting the unfortunate creature, Sophie was already losing herself in the music again.

In her dream, The DeModie's melody played all day long, leading Sophie through dark labyrinths and past gruesome shadows. At no time did she feel fear, for Luca would always look out for her. If she fell, he was there. If the shadows came too close, he drove them away. When the music faded, he gave her new strength.

She was abruptly roused from her sleep. "Hey, Sophie! What are you doing?"

Irritated, she blinked and tried to rise from the mists of her dream.

Jonas was standing bent over her bed, shaking her shoulder. "You can't keep sleeping now."

"Why not?" asked Sophie, terribly tired. There was no way it was time to be up again. She would have heard her alarm clock.

The answer came promptly. "Because you're already late."

"The curse!" she cried, startled. Had she slept through nightfall?

Annoyed, Jonas let go of her. "Forget about the bloody curse! Your audition starts in half an hour. If we hurry, we might make it before they start."

Relieved, Sophie let herself sink back into the pillows. She still had time before nightfall. Luca was safe. "Oh, you mean the audition." She remembered it vaguely now. "Why didn't you say so? You gave me a fright."

"Sophie!" Jonas cried, horrified. "We have to go."

The loud words hurt her ears. "We'll never make it. I'd have to get warmed up and everything. If they notice that I've only just showed up, I'll already be dismissed, anyway." She pulled the covers over her head.

Jonas wouldn't leave her alone, though. "You'll also be dismissed if you don't show up." He pulled the blanket off her head again. "You promised."

He fell silent. The audition seemed forgotten. Slowly, he pushed the blanket down a little more. "What's that?"

Irritated, Sophie looked down at her arm, which showed a grotesque bite mark among countless other bruises and scratches. She could barely remember how it had got there. Last night was nothing more than wild snapshots in her mind. "There was a lot going on last night, I think. You know how it is."

"No, I don't know," Jonas answered in a hard voice.

Annoyed, Sophie looked at him. Of course, he had no idea, removed from life as he was. "Since I'm not allowed to sleep, at least let me take a shower." She was still wearing the dress she had gone dancing in. Sleep had wrinkled it.

When she tried to get up, however, Jonas held her by the arm. "Sophie, this can't go on. Don't you realise what's happening?"

Now it was she who glared at him. "Will you please stop acting like my father?"

Groaning, Jonas rolled his eyes and let her go. As Sophie rubbed her sore spots, he continued to pester her, "You need to give him up, Sophie."

There was no question who he meant. "I'm not giving up on Luca. You should know that by now!"

Jonas didn't answer right away. Instead, he gasped for air. When he finally found his voice, it seemed to Sophie he'd been saving these words for months. "The only curse is that you run into that stupid club every night and risk life and limb. Look at you! You're asleep in your clothes. You went to bed with make-up on." Unconsciously, her fingers found her face. "Those shoes you wear are falling off your feet. Looking at your arms, you'd think you'd been mugged. Where was Luca when you were scratched and bitten?"

He had held her in his arms and smiled lovingly at her. That was the only thing she could remember clearly. "He was with me."

Jonas snorted. "Wow, wonderful! And he didn't care. Or was it him who did this to you?"

Again, he reached for Sophie's arm, but this time she pulled away in time. "No! Luca loves me. He would never do such a thing."

"Luca doesn't love you. He loves the way out you're promising him!" Jonas yelled at her.

Shocked, they stared at each other. He had never been loud before, had never shown so much passion in all the time he'd lived here.

Obviously, he regretted his outburst instantly, because he suddenly screwed up his face and huffed. The tension fell off him. But before Jonas could apologise, she rushed past him, determined to take a shower.

"And you don't love him either," he called after her, almost desperately.

Again, Sophie stopped. Slowly, she turned to face him in the hallway. "What makes you think that? I love Luca more than anything. I'm counting the days until I can finally take him with me." Outside, she heard the rain drumming on the roof.

Jonas had calmed down, but was still frowning heavily. "No," he contradicted her in a firm voice. "You're counting the days until you finally don't have to dance with him anymore."

His words took her breath away. All at once, Sophie felt dizzy.

"You can't tell me that you're happy right now. But I guess you don't need to bother with your issues so long as you're dancing with Luca."

"I don't follow you, Jonas," Sophie admitted wearily.

"Then I'll explain it to you," he said. "You dream of being a ballerina, don't you? But all of a sudden, you no longer care about the audition."

Sophie didn't like where this was going. "I just overslept, that's all," she defended herself again.

Jonas shook his head vehemently. "Then why didn't you set an alarm clock?"

She'd forgotten when she fell into bed this morning, completely exhausted.

"You're always running away, Sophie. You don't want this year to end. If it did, you'd finally have to face your past. Finally admit that you're afraid. That you're afraid of being on stage."

Sophie couldn't help but laugh nervously. "You're crazy, Jonas."

"I know what it means to run away. You showed me." He sounded so terribly serious and grown up. "But it doesn't help. It always catches up with you, and the only way you can beat it is to face it."

"You're one to talk," she retorted.

Unapologetically, Jonas admitted, "Yes, that's right. I'm one to talk. That's why I understand what you're doing. You're clinging to your past, unable to take a step into the future. That's why you like Luca. Because time stands still with him."

Defiantly, Sophie began to shake her head.

For the second time this afternoon, Jonas' voice grew louder. "You can't even manage to put on sensible shoes."

The broken shoes she stoically tied around her feet every night lay on the floor between them. The new ones were still untouched in their box. "I need the shoes," she heard herself say. "I can't stand the nights without them."

"That's bullshit!" Jonas seemed about to despair. "They're just shoes. Completely danced through, dirty, broken shoes."

"They were my mum's!" Sophie exclaimed in horror. She suddenly felt the need to pick up the shoes and press them to her chest.

Jonas sighed and began to massage his temples. More gently, he continued, "I know, but I keep wondering if they're not to blame for all this."

Out of exasperation, she raised her voice, "For what?"

"That you can't stop dancing with Luca!" When she shook her head in confusion, Jonas explained, "When I was at The DeModie, I saw a wall with dozens of shoes hanging on it. They were all broken, but there was one free nail at the end. The spot for yours."

His words made her uncomfortable. Anxiously, Sophie took a step back. "What nonsense is this?" She shook her head. "The shoes aren't cursed; Luca is."

"Then wear different ones!" Jonas suggested, stepping closer.

"Why would I?"

With a snort, he stopped. "Leave them here, Sophie. I know what they mean to you, but they won't bring your mother back. And neither can Luca."

Her eyes burned and her throat tightened painfully. "What is it with you and Luca all the time? It's not his fault he was cursed." Tears ran down her cheeks. "He's sweet and kind. He protects me."

With nerve-wracking patience, Jonas explained, "But that doesn't add up. If Luca has been cursed to spend his life in hell, how does he manage to keep all these other... *creatures* at bay that abuse you night after night?"

"He's a prince," Sophie said stubbornly.

Jonas shook his head. "He's a charlatan. A liar. He's just making this curse up, so you'll dutifully run to him every night. And your shoes carry you to him."

Angry at her tears, Sophie bit her lips. She tried for sarcasm. "Because The DeModie already has a place reserved for them?"

"Why don't you ask Luca about it? I can't wait to hear his answer. He'll probably just tell you a little more about the terrible curse that's been plaguing him."

Sophie wrapped her arms around herself. "You're just jealous."

Jonas sighed. "It's not that—I'm not the one wearing rose-tinted glasses around Luca. Because while you're looking worse by the day and throwing your life away, Luca remains the shining prince in armour. They don't bite him, do they? He doesn't get attacked like you do."

The doubts gnawed at her more and more, but she couldn't give in. She had promised Luca, after all. "You *are* jealous. Do you think I don't see how obsessed you are with me?"

At last, Jonas closed his mouth.

"Do you know how much it sucks to hear all the time that I'm the only thing in your life that means anything to you?"

"It sucks?" he asked helplessly.

"Call it exhausting, for all I care," she exclaimed loudly, throwing her arms in the air. "I always have to be perfect for you, always have to function. You put me on this damn pedestal and then get mad when I'm not what you want me to be." She saw him shake his head in shock, but she had finally found her anger. "I'm not perfect! And I don't want to be your anchor, or whatever you see in me." Breathing heavily, Sophie braced her hands on her hips. "I just want to live my life, and I want to do it without anyone looking out for me all the time."

Jonas regarded her with big puppy eyes. "I'm sorry if you felt I was pressuring you or—"

Rudely, Sophie interrupted him before he could start whining again, "But that's what you're doing. Your whole presence here puts insane pressure on me. Not only do I have to dance with Luca every night, no! During the day, I also have to make sure you don't sink back into your nightmares."

Jonas visibly stiffened.

"And at the risk of my life, too."

"I never meant to—" began Jonas.

Sophie silenced him again. "I really have a lot of patience and also a lot of understanding, but at some point, enough is enough. You can't tell me I'm ruining my life when you're the one not in control of theirs. Who's the one that can't let go of the past? Who doesn't know how to live anymore, and above all, runs away all the time?"

Disparagingly, she looked him up and down. "What did you tell your parents at Christmas? You might visit someday?"

She snorted. "We both know that day will never be. You just hope they'll stop asking about you. It probably makes you uncomfortable that they won't just let you go. That you still owe them to stay alive, and can't just give up."

"Sophie, please." It sounded pitiful.

"No!" Sophie jutted her chin in the air. "I've had enough of this. Either you get your shit together for once or you leave me alone. But stop this jealousy crap!"

Jonas moved on to pleading, "Sophie, I know I hurt you. I also know that I'm not a particularly good role model. I'm a terrible one, in fact. There is no doubt about that. But I know that Luca is not good for you." Frustrated, Sophie stamped her foot, whereupon Jonas hastily continued, "I'm not perfect, not by a long shot, but at least I'm human. I'm not so sure about Luca and his brothers, after everything you've said."

"Jonas, you're being ridiculous!" What else could she do to make him finally realise how much nonsense he was currently spouting? "You've only seen Luca twice. I *know* him."

"No, you don't," Jonas shot back almost as desperate. "How old is he?" The question threw her completely. "Where is he from? What country did he live in? What does he want to do after his redemption?"

Hesitantly, Sophie reached for the only answer she could grasp. "Dance with me."

For a moment, Jonas just nodded in silence. His face was lined with despair, just as Frederick's had been back in September. "And you don't think he's just saying that because it's what you want to hear?"

She shook her head. "Luca loves dancing just as much as I do."

"I see." A bitter edge had entered his voice. Jonas bent down, picked up the broken shoes, and stroked the ruined satin fabric. "And you do all this for him of your own free will? Destroying your body and probably ruining any future in ballet for yourself."

He nodded at her feet. Inevitably, Sophie looked down. Her knuckles were red and bruised. Generations of blisters overlapped each other. A dull pain lingered in them that only Tomas' cocktails could quell.

"Yes," she said, even though there was no confidence to go with it. Luca was worth it. He had to be.

"I can't stop you from going to Luca, but I don't want your shoes hanging on that nail at some point." He turned away and walked slowly to the door.

Sophie watched his back with suspicion. "What are you doing?"

He answered as he slipped on his shoes and took his jacket, "I'm taking the shoes up to your father. He can look after them while you dance with Luca—in sensible shoes."

Suddenly, she felt ice cold. Her chest tightened painfully and her legs almost gave way. "You're going too far, Jonas."

Guiltily, he lowered his head and opened the door. "Probably, but I can't stand by and watch you run to your doom."

At last, her legs responded, and Sophie rushed towards Jonas. "Give me back my shoes!" she demanded, snatching at them.

Jonas was quicker. His face hardened, and he stepped out into the rain. "You'll get them back in May, Sophie. Or do you want them completely ruined?" Quietly, he added, "And you with them?"

For a moment, Sophie stood rooted to the spot in the doorway. The rain had turned the once white blanket of snow into filthy slush.

Jonas pulled up the collar of his jacket and trudged over to the main house.

"Jonas!" shrieked Sophie loudly and rushed after him. She barely got three steps before the rain had soaked her to the bone. The cold bit into her bare toes as she ran through the icy mud.

Dismayed, Jonas looked at her and snatched up her shoes at the last moment before she could reach for them. "My goodness, Sophie!"

"Give. Me. My. Shoes!" she commanded, yanking roughly on his arm.

"You're out of your mind." Jonas lifted the shoes even higher.

In desperation, Sophie jabbed her elbow into his ribs and clung to his arm.

Jonas doubled over with a groan, but caught himself far too quickly. In no time at all, he had taken the shoes in his right hand, lunged, and flung them from him in a high arc.

Screaming, Sophie pushed herself off him and after them. She soon found one. It was hanging between the bare branches of a hedge, and when she pulled on it, the ribbon snapped. The sound hurt her almost physically. Miserably slow, she set about freeing the other ribbon from the thorns with clammy fingers, not minding the scratches she received in the process.

Finally, Sophie managed to free the shoe from the undergrowth and looked around helplessly for a second. Out of the corner of her eye, she saw Jonas step out of the door with his never-unpacked travel bag over his shoulder. Without making any move to help her, he stopped and watched her.

Cursing, she dug for the shoe in the icy mud with stiff fingers before finally spotting it near the wall behind the bushes. Without thinking, she chose the direct route and was annoyed when the thorns pinned her down. Her wet dress tore audibly, and at last, Sophie stumbled towards the shoe. Relieved, she sank to her knees in front of it and picked it up.

Behind her, she now heard smacking footsteps in the mud. In the thick veil of rain, she could barely make out Jonas' face. His words, however, she heard with painful clarity. "I'm sorry." He seemed to search for more words, but none passed his lips. Shame burned in Sophie's cheeks as she pressed her shoes close to her heart. Finally, he sighed. "Goodbye, Sophie."

As he turned away, the words penetrated deep into her heart, and with a start, Sophie realised what he meant. She wanted to call after him, wanted him to stay, but her teeth were chattering too much, and no sound came out. She had no choice but to watch his outline disappear into the rain.

Only with great difficulty, Sophie managed to pick herself up afterwards and stagger back into the house. Her head was strangely dull and empty all of a sudden, but her feet carried her straight to the shower. Even the lukewarm water burned like hell on her hypothermic skin, and she barely registered she was still wearing the dress she had danced in with Luca yesterday.

Luca.

Soon, she'd have to be on her way to him. She couldn't risk losing him, too. Who else would she have left then?

Changement

"Hey, Mum."

The tray hit the floor with a thud. Jonas winced as the teacups and pot shattered and hot tea splashed across the tiles. He struggled to fight down a fit while his mother went into shock, her hand half raised to her mouth.

A moment later, he heard his father's heavy footsteps. "Is everything all ri—" He stuck his head into the hallway and paused, puzzled. "Jonas?"

Jonas shook his head, fighting down the lump in his throat. "No, nothing's right."

His mother threw herself around his neck and hugged him tightly, as if she'd never let him go again. "There you are. We were worried about you." Her hands roamed over his face, making sure he was truly there. Then she pressed a kiss to his forehead.

"Come, sit down, my boy. I'll clean this up in a minute." As she grabbed Jonas' hand to pull him into the living room, his gaze met his father's.

His father's frowned and patted him briefly on the shoulders before asking, "What's the matter? Do you need money?"

"Henning!" his wife said, aghast. "Let Jonas sit down first."

Jonas swallowed and forced himself not to look at the shards still lying on the floor. He could already hear the rattle of machine guns in the background. His mouth went dry as dust. "Can I have something to drink?" he asked as he took a seat at the dining table.

A cursory glance around the living room told him that not much had changed during his absence. His mother still displayed the family pictures and hand-painted plates she had inherited from her grandmother. The TV was running, showing a football game.

His mother made her way to the kitchen. "Sure. What would you like? Coke? Water?"

"A beer?" Actually, he preferred something stronger, but Jonas was embarrassed enough as it was to ask for alcohol.

"I can also open a wine," came the reply from the kitchen, "to celebrate, so to speak."

Jonas knew there was nothing to celebrate. But it was alcohol. Meekly, he replied, "Okay."

Restlessly, he looked around the familiar living room one more time, suppressing the urge to get up and check the corners. The pictures on the walls showed two laughing boys who seemed like strangers to him. Had there ever been a time before the war?

Looking up, he noticed his father's critical gaze. "Well?"

"I..." Jonas wished he already had a glass in his hand to hold on to. "I need help."

His father snorted, unsurprised. Before he could say anything, however, Jonas' mother returned and placed the bottle and three glasses on the table. "Why don't you pour while I quickly clean up the shards?"

Shards.

Shards and dust.

Jonas struggled to keep his composure. His fingers clawed into the table, and he gasped. He couldn't give in to the visions now. Not in their presence.

"Jonas?" He could clearly hear the fear in the question. Sophie had been afraid too, even if she'd only admitted it at the end.

The thought of Sophie still hurt. He had been about to turn around and go back to her three times on his way home. He wanted to explain himself to her, beg her forgiveness, find a way to turn back time. So much had been said that he could never take back.

The memory of her pleading look pained him so much that it drove away the visions of war and made Jonas think clearly again. He blinked and saw that his parents hadn't moved at all.

Swallowing, Jonas reached for the wine bottle and uncorked it. The movement made his father breathe a sigh of relief and he gently took the bottle from Jonas' shaking hands and poured. "What's wrong?"

"Nothing," Jonas murmured and took a sip of the heavy red wine. "It's... just a memory." All at once, despair threatened to overtake him. He was unable to meet his parents' eyes. Instead, he regarded the dark red liquid in his glass. "Like blood," he whispered.

The shards were forgotten. His mother sat down beside him and grabbed his hand. "Honey, I don't understand. What blood?"

Hastily, Jonas downed the glass so he wouldn't have to think about the last time he had seen so much fresh blood. Despite his mother's firm grip, his hands shook uncontrollably. All at once, the words burst out of him, "Everywhere I go, I see these images. Memories of the war." He buried his free hand in his hair, clawing into the skin of his head. "They just won't leave me alone. Every night the same nightmares. Bursting windows, dust, blood everywhere. An insane amount of blood, dirt encrusted, dusty, fresh. And then," he swallowed hard, "then come the screams.

"It's like I'm still there. Like I never came home. I thought the nightmares would eventually subside, maybe even go away, but they don't. They keep getting worse and I don't know what to do anymore." At last, Jonas jerked his chin up and looked directly at his parents. "I need help. Real help. From a psychiatrist or, I don't know, someone."

For some time, no one said a word. Jonas could hear the dishwasher running in the kitchen and a pipe crackling somewhere in the house. Almost as if lost in thought, his mother rubbed the back of his hand with her fingers. Her eyes shimmered suspiciously.

Finally, she smiled and said, despite the approaching tears, "Well, you're home now. We'll get it sorted, Jonas. I'm sure we will."

Jonas was nowhere near as sure of that.

Jonas was sorry he had burdened his parents with this. All evening, his father hadn't said another word. Instead, he had observed him and brooded in silence. As if he was just waiting for Jonas to reveal it had all been a bad joke. His mother, on the other hand, had cried a lot and kept reassuring him that everything would be all right.

Now they were arguing about which of them was to blame for his condition.

Jonas lay in his childhood bed and could only hear isolated words through the thick walls. It was enough for him to curse himself for letting them in on it. After all, he had never wanted them to blame themselves because of his issues.

Still, he needed their help. He would never dare go to a psychiatrist on his own. And his mother had promised to accompany him.

"...always coddled him, then..."

His stomach tightened at his father's words, which immediately triggered his mental carousel. How many times had he been ashamed of his weakness? No one else in his troop suffered as much as he did. Why had it hit him of all people?

He knew only one thing for sure. That it was all down to him and not his mother's loving upbringing or his father's high standards. Jonas wished he had the strength to stand up, go down, and tell them that they weren't to blame for this. Instead, he listened in silence while his mother burst into tears again, waiting for nightmarish sleep to release him.

The next day, his father took him aside for what he called "a real man's talk". On the terrace, he lit a cigar, offering Jonas one as well. Jonas declined, never having liked the smell.

"Now listen, boy. I don't know what it was exactly you experienced in Afghanistan, but you got the Cross of Honour for your service. That means you're a hero. You—"

"It means I served five years," Jonas replied bitterly. He had always felt the honour was like a slap in the face. An empty symbol without any meaning. All because he'd survived five years in the army. Yet, here he was, still struggling with it now.

His father sighed, "Oh, Jonas. You're taking this all far too much to heart. Look, your brother was in Afghanistan too. He was even in Kabul when that madman blew himself up."

Explosion. Dust. Blood. Jonas bit his lips until he tasted his own blood. He had known his father wouldn't understand. Who wanted a weakling in the family?

His father continued to press on, "What I'm trying to say is that you just have to learn how to put this behind you. It's just another head thing of yours. Once you stop telling yourself that you're somehow damaged, you'll be fine. It's just memories, Jonas. They can't hurt you. Look at Felix or me! Nothing like that ever happened to us. And you know why? Because when we came home, we came home. We left the war where it was."

"I didn't choose this," Jonas said, taking a deep breath to keep from whining. He didn't want to break down again. It would only confirm his father's assessment of his weakness. Piece by piece, he built up a wall to guard himself against the words that followed.

"I told you right away not to throw everything away like that. If you had stayed in the Bundeswehr, or even better, gone straight back out into the field... You'd be amazed. The whole thing would take care of itself. Without the help of any quacks."

Under the table, Jonas clenched his hands around his knees so they wouldn't twitch treacherously. The very idea of having to go back drove a cold sweat to his brow. "Mhm," was all he managed.

"Maybe it'll help you if you go back? You know we don't give up on our people." His father drew on the cigar.

Jonas could only stare at him in horror. In his experience, they had abandoned so many. Maybe not soldiers, but civilians. Countless women and children with empty hands and wide eyes. Finally, he whispered, "I don't need to go back there. I never came home."

His father's eyes widened, and Jonas turned his head to the side. He knew the terror in them well enough.

—

His father's words still haunted Jonas as he sat in the waiting room of the psychiatrist his mother had chosen for him. In contrast to all the doctors he'd met, the practice rather resembled a comfortable living room. Expansive leather armchairs invited him to linger, a large aquarium bubbled pleasantly in a corner, and potted plants livened up the room.

Jonas' gaze, however, was fixed firmly on the light carpet. His fingers dug into the fabric of his trousers just above the knee. Next to him, his mother was leafing through the journals on display. Every now and then, she drew his attention to an article, but Jonas had no more than a fleeting glance for them. His thoughts were too much on the upcoming conversation and everything that had brought him here.

Now that he was here, he wished he were far away. He had no idea what to expect, didn't even know if he should hope for medication or not. It would be nice if there was a miracle cure that would simply make his nightmares disappear. But that would be the same as Sophie's cocktails and he had seen how little those had helped. Jonas wanted more than just a plaster.

Still, the idea of having to deal with his experiences again frightened him. Filling out the questionnaire had already proven difficult for him, and in a moment, he would meet a stranger he had to confide in. "I'm going to get another drink," Jonas announced and walked over to the water dispenser.

"Again?" his mother asked, looking at him anxiously. It was the third time he had stood up.

"I'm thirsty," he explained redundantly.

Smiling softly, his mother patted the seat beside her. "You're nervous. I remember how many water bottles I had to clear out of your room when you were studying for your high school diploma."

A high school diploma that had turned out to be completely useless. Sighing, Jonas returned to the couch with the cup. "I just hope this will do some good."

Comfortingly, his mother placed a hand on his leg. "I wish I could help you, but you're right. You do need professional help. You know that yourself. Believe me, everything will be fine. And I'll be there every single step of the way." The slight pressure disappeared from his thigh, and she turned back to her magazine.

Jonas continued to stare at the carpet, ruminating on things he couldn't change.

His thoughts lingered on Sophie as the door at the end of the room opened. "Mr Grienkamp?"

Jonas immediately jumped to his feet. The psychiatrist was a stern-looking woman in her mid-forties. She had the questionnaire in her hand, which he noticed instantly, but her face didn't show what she thought about it. Instead, a friendly smile lit up her features as she walked up to him and held out her hand. "Doctor Hannemann, pleased to meet you. And this must be your mother. We spoke on the phone?"

"Elke Grienkamp, yes." Enthusiastically, she shook the psychiatrist's hand. "But I can wait outside if that's better."

Instead of at his mother, Doctor Hannemann looked at Jonas. "Well, that's for Mr Grienkamp to decide. What would you prefer?"

He was embarrassed about the fact that he was a grown man going to the doctor with his mother, but without her at his side, he would have turned back before he'd reached the door. "If you don't mind, I'd like her to come with me," he replied, wetting his dry lips. "We're not really getting into anything today, are we?"

"Not much, no. We'll just discuss the possible course of treatment and then you'll have to decide on how to proceed. But come on, let's go into the office first." With an inviting gesture, Doctor Hannemann led them both into her treatment room.

In front of the large wide window was a small seating area with the same comfortable leather furniture as the waiting room. Her desk was further back and was obviously not used during the meetings. Instead, they took a seat in front of the window. For a brief moment, his mother squeezed Jonas' knees before looking around the room. "It's really nice in here. Very bright."

"Thank you. I always find it makes the hours a little more pleasant." As the two made brief small talk, Jonas let his gaze drift around the room, checking for possible exits. Behind the curtain stood a shadow he couldn't place. The sight made his heart beat faster and his hands damp.

"Mr Grienkamp, may I call you by your first name? I always find it easier to talk to my patients that way."

Caught off guard, Jonas looked up and clicked his heels together. He nodded, but his eyes kept sliding back to the curtain. "Sure."

Without comment, Doctor Hannemann stood up and pulled the fabric aside so he could get a glimpse of the floor lamp hidden behind it. As if that was always part of her routine, she sat back down and, glancing at the questionnaire, continued, "Alright, Jonas. I've just read through what you're here for. I commend you for taking this step. It's exactly the right thing to do. I can read about your symptoms here, but I'd like to know more about you first. Tell me a little about what you do, what interests you. Whatever you want," she concluded with a sweeping gesture.

I was at war. Dust, rubble, blood. The images assailed Jonas immediately, and his hands began to tremble. He knew that wasn't what she had asked. Knew there had to be more to him than his past as a soldier. Once there had been a lot there. But now there was only the eternal war and… "Sophie."

Looking up, his gaze met his mother's slightly puzzled face. Her short laugh sounded nervous. "Who's Sophie? Do I know her?" Glancing at the therapist, she quickly covered her mouth. "Sorry."

Doctor Hannemann smiled fleetingly. "That's alright. I was going to ask the same question."

Jonas hesitated. Sophie had been such a big part of his life over the last few months, it seemed weird no one else knew her. "Um, a friend." he replied. "We lived together for a while until..." Again, he paused. He saw the red marks on Sophie's neck in his mind. "Until it got worse."

"Hmm." Doctor Hannemann sat up a little straighter. "Do you want to tell me more about it?"

Immediately, Jonas shook his head. "No, honestly, I don't." Especially not in front of his mother. The psychiatrist's look was very understanding. "I just have these nightmares, and if I don't wake up, I get lost in them, and then I don't recognise Sophie."

"I understand." Now she leaned slightly forward. "Your dream are pretty bad, aren't they?"

Joylessly, Jonas laughed. "Nah, I could spend hours with them."

"Jonas!" His mother struggled for composure. "Please take this seriously."

With a little smirk, Doctor Hannemann replied, "Well, I'm glad to hear that, because it will make my job a lot easier."

Uneasily, Jonas slid around in his chair. He didn't actually want to spend more time with nightmares, living or recounting them.

"I would like to know more about you and Sophie at some point, but I realise that you have other things on your mind at the moment."

From a pile, she took an information booklet and slid it across the table. The title meant nothing to Jonas and only made him frown. "Given the severe impairments caused by your trauma, I'd like to try Prolonged Exposure Therapy, using a cognitive approach. That means we'll deal intensively with your trauma," the psychiatrist explained.

Jonas' fingernails dug deep into his palms. In the course of the conversation, he had moved to the edge of the chair. His mother's presence was the only thing keeping him from getting up and leaving. It was her who asked with incredible calm, "And what does that mean exactly?"

"In PE Therapy, Jonas will tell me all the details of his experiences and try to mentally put himself back into the situation. I will, of course, be at his side during this."

Shocked, Jonas opened his eyes and stared at the therapist. The well-known images came flooding back already.

"The whole thing is recorded and has to be listened to again and again at home. In this way, he is slowly desensitised to the trauma. With the cognitive..."

The rest of her words were lost in the roaring in Jonas' ears. His mouth had become horribly dry, and his nails were burning into his skin. The thought of having to imagine what he had experienced over and over again almost drove him mad.

"Jonas? Say something, Jonas."

With difficulty, Jonas fought his way out of the whirlpool of memories and back to the surface.

"That sounds quite promising, doesn't it?" his mother sought confirmation, smiling vaguely.

Jonas searched for help with the psychiatrist.

Dr Hannemann adjusted her glasses before admitting, "I'll be honest with you. This will be anything but easy. You may get to the point where you want to give up and never come back. But if you want to get past this, we have our work cut out for us."

Jonas swallowed hard. He suddenly wasn't so sure he wanted to get past it.

Meanwhile, Doctor Hannemann continued, "Let me be frank. I've been watching you for a while now. You seem to find it very difficult to focus on the here and now. Even a small thing, a word, a single image is enough to trigger you. You appear completely overwhelmed, and it won't get better if you don't do something about it. Only worse." She took a deep breath. "I want to help you find some coping mechanisms. I've had a few patients who've had wonderful results with PE Therapy, including two soldiers. But I need your help with this. We can't do this without your cooperation and the time you have to invest in the therapy at home. And you want to get better, don't you? You no longer want to be afraid of hurting yourself or others. Sophie, for example."

His mouth was so parched it hurt, but Jonas finally brought himself to nod. He would do anything for Sophie.

"Good, then we'll make some appointments right now and I'll give you some reading to do." This time, she handed him a pamphlet on post-traumatic stress disorder.

Jonas stared at the letters until they blurred before his eye. Three words that summed up the miserable life he led. It felt as if the weight on his shoulders had suddenly become unbearably heavy.

His own scream echoed from the speakers, followed by sobs that stifled any further words. Shaking, Jonas sat in front of the computer, the whiskey bottle in his hand, and took another sip. In a moment, he would beg Doctor Hannemann not to have to say any more, and they would break off the session.

Before that could happen, the door to his room opened, and his brother Felix entered unexpectedly, cautiously glancing behind.

Hectically, Jonas reached for the mouse and switched off the recording. Due to the sudden motion, whiskey sloshed over his fingers and dripped onto the keyboard. "What... what are you doing here?"

"Dad called me. He wants me to talk sense into you or something like that." Felix didn't sound like he even considered doing as much. He looked at Jonas anxiously, his hands on his hips. No sooner had he spotted the bottle than he reached for it. "Man, don't let Mum see that!"

Reluctantly, Jonas released the bottle. "There's no point, anyway."

Sighing, Felix put the whisky down on the dresser and sat down opposite him. "You've only been at it for a month, Jonas. Things like this don't happen overnight."

"What would you know about it?" Jonas turned his face away. Felix didn't need to see how much his words hurt him. His eyes burned and his jaw ached so hard he clenched his teeth.

His brother had no idea what it was like to relive the war over and over again. Jonas had sought therapy to stop being tormented by the nightmare visions. Instead, he was forced to recall them to himself every day now.

"Honestly?" Felix looked at the door and then leaned forward, forcing Jonas to meet his eye. "Let's keep this between us though, okay? I almost lost a comrade to PTSD back then."

Shocked, Jonas's eyes widened, and his breathing quickened. "You never told me about that."

Felix shrugged his shoulders. "It's not like anyone talks about those things. You know how it is. They give you the info, but of course no one expects to get sick. After all, we're men, and soldiers at that."

Jonas vaguely remembered the moment during his basic training when they had been told about the therapy options available to them. At the time, he had laughed about it because the instructor had made fun of the over-correct regulations. As if that could never happen to them.

"Well, Matze never said anything either and then... well, a pill overdose. We all felt horrible."

At his brother's words, Jonas' chest tightened painfully.

"We didn't hear from him for months until I met him by chance in Hamburg. That's when he told me about the therapy."

"PE?" asked Jonas doubtfully. The oppressive feeling in his chest almost took his breath away.

Felix nodded. "Yes, that one." He snorted and shook his head. "Honestly, Jonas, I wouldn't have wanted to trade places with him. Experiencing Kabul once was bad enough. To experience it over and over again... I couldn't." Jonas hadn't been in Kabul at the time of the attack, but he knew what it was like when houses collapsed and people ran screaming into the streets.

All at once, Felix tapped him on the shoulder. The brief touch prevented the false memories from becoming too real. "But you can do this. You'll get through this, and I'll be here for you, okay?"

"What about your girlfriend?" Jonas asked, mostly to get away from the distressing images of war in his mind.

"I told her it was an emergency. I'll stay as long as you need me. And I mean that. You can always come to me and talk. Or not talk." He stood up and picked up the whiskey bottle. "But don't drink. That only adds one more problem."

Jonas sighed. He knew that alcohol was no solution, but it was the only thing that made the recordings bearable. He stared out the window. If only Felix would leave faster.

"Alright." Jonas felt another comforting handshake on his shoulder. "Keep your chin up, kid. You got away from them once. They won't get you now. You just have to hang on a little longer. It'll get better, I promise."

~

It didn't get better.

"Blood. There was so much blood. Everywhere." He could see it, on his hands, on his clothes, the pools in the street. The memory dug into his guts like red-hot iron. Tormented, Jonas looked up at his therapist.

How calmly she sat there, her gaze understanding and yet so impassive. She hadn't been there. She couldn't understand how bad it had been for him.

"I couldn't help them," Jonas groaned breathlessly. "No one. Not my comrades and not the locals. There were civilians there. Children!" He still saw their eyes. They had begged him. Like Sophie. But he had been unable to do anything. Now they were dead.

Everywhere he looked, bodies piled up. The dust hung thick in the air. Fear crept up Jonas' spine. What if they were discovered now? He didn't even have enough ammunition in his rifle.

"...at an important point here, Jonas." Doctor Hannemann's voice filtered through to him with difficulty. It prevented him from listening to the footsteps in the darkness that were approaching their hiding place. "Tell me what happened after that."

Jonas slapped his hands over his ears and shook his head. He didn't want to think about it any longer. Didn't want to relive the death of his best friend. Didn't want to endure the shame of how he had pressed himself next to the latter's dead body, pleading to everyone and no one that they wouldn't find him while his shoulder burned like fire.

Instead, he jumped up and rushed out the door. Behind him, he could hear Dr Hannemann calling his name, but Jonas didn't dare turn around again. He had to get out of here. Had to get away from all this.

He made it as far as the stairwell before throwing up, because the memories continued to pile up on him unchecked. The empty look in Philipp's eyes, even though his body was still warm. The child in the street, blood streaming down his forehead. The cramped hand sticking out of the pile of rubble.

Groaning, Jonas clutched the banister as he emptied the contents of his stomach, wordlessly pleading for it to stop. Under no circumstances could he endure the images one more time.

⁓

Enraged, Jonas threw the USB stick with his recordings against the wall and stomped on it until the connector was bent. Then he dragged out his travel bag and threw things into it at random. He would stop the therapy, that much was certain. It had only made things worse and exposed the worst of his memories. Those that he had buried so painstakingly.

Philipp's dead eyes and the feeling of his body beside him had stayed with him all the way home. In his head, the screams rang, leaving him with no clear thought, only endless rage. Rage at the war, rage at Doctor Hannemann, rage at himself. When Jonas found his drawing pad under the last T-shirt, he threw that against the wall too. The sheets flew around the room.

The swirling paper had a strangely calming effect on him. He couldn't connect it with any of his bloody memories. Instead, he stood there panting, his hands clenched into fists. His cheek twitched while his throat tightened, and all at once, the tears came. At first, they ran slowly, still tickling at the corner of his mouth, then they burst forth. A strangled sound escaped his throat and his knees went weak.

Jonas hardly noticed how the door opened and his brother crossed the room in quick steps. When he felt Felix's arms around him, he was already crying his eyes out, unable to say a word. His legs had long since given way and he held onto Felix's shoulders like a drowning man. Reassuringly, his brother stroked his back and hummed comfortingly in his ear. "It's going to be alright, Jonas. It's going to be alright."

Eventually, Jonas drew enough breath to speak aloud the terrible thought that had been lurking deep beneath all the memories for so long. "I can't take it anymore. I just can't take it. I wish it had been me then."

"I know," his brother whispered. "I know." He didn't forbid Jonas to think about it, didn't dismiss it as nonsense, didn't despair about it. Felix just accepted it for what it was, and for a brief moment, Jonas allowed himself to actually think about what it meant.

It was absurd. The moment he put himself in Philipp's place, he knew he didn't want this. Being dead was absolutely unacceptable. How else could he have met Sophie or ever left the war behind? He didn't want his life to end with

Afghanistan. That wasn't what he'd been fighting for. For his family, for Sophie, but most importantly for himself.

Sniffling, he detached himself from his brother and wiped his face with his sleeve. Felix handed him a handkerchief and Jonas blew his nose. His gaze fell on the sheets of paper at his feet, on Sophie and the buildings he'd designed an impossible number of years ago. Lost in thought, he bent down and looked at the drawing of an art gallery. "Do you think I could manage a degree someday?" He had already blown the last attempt.

Felix stepped closer and looked over his shoulder. "Architecture? Why not? You know you can draw. And you always liked buildings." His voice sounded strange, as if he too was on the verge of tears. "And you'll soon get to grips with the other stuff, too."

Jonas didn't want to think about the other stuff. For the first time in a long while, the memories were kept at bay, and if he had his way, they'd stay that way. Carefully, he began to pick up the drawings again. Maybe he would pick up sketching again.

Beside him, Felix went down on his knees to help him. He held up one of the drawings and asked, "Is that Sophie?"

Of course, it was her. From all around the room, she was looking at Jonas. "How do you know about her?"

"Mum mentioned her," Felix replied, comparing the different pictures. "She does ballet?"

"You talked about me?" Jonas asked instead.

Apologetically, Felix looked up at him. "What do you think? We're all worried about you, aren't we? Mum and Dad are completely overwhelmed. I've tried to explain what you're going through, but I don't really understand it either. Not like you do."

Jonas nodded a little. It was what he would have done.

His gaze fell on Sophie's likeness. It showed her during one of her endless pirouettes, her arms high above her head. The sight made him sad. He shouldn't have left her in a quarrel. At the very least, he owed her an explanation. And at that moment, he knew he had to return to her. Not now, but eventually.

"Yes, that's Sophie. But don't get Mum's hopes up! She has a boyfriend." One he didn't trust one bit, but Jonas didn't tell his brother that. Luca was who Sophie had chosen, and nothing would change that.

Felix shrugged his shoulders. "Too bad. She's quite pretty."

"Yes. Yes, she is." A smile slid across Jonas's lips. "And you should see her dance. I've never seen anything so magical."

Somehow, he told Felix all about Sophie. How she danced and laughed, how she raged when she felt she'd been treated unfairly, and also how much she'd feared him after he'd attacked her in his frenzy. After he told Felix how they'd parted, the latter looked thoughtful. "Do you know what helped Matze back then? Along with the therapy, of course."

Jonas shook his head.

"Writing. He wrote down everything he saw, felt, thought. Every little detail. I never read the stuff—no one has—but he claimed it freed him. Even more than talking to the psychiatrist, because he could never really say everything there. But he could confide in the paper." He nodded to the badly damaged pad. "Perhaps that could help you as well."

Jonas didn't hold out much hope, but he swore to himself that he would give it a try at least. He owed Sophie that much, after all. Maybe, one day, he could even explain to her what was going on inside of him.

"Think about it." Felix patted him encouragingly on the shoulder and stood up again. "I'll go and calm Mum down before she goes mad."

Minutes after his brother had disappeared, Jonas was still sitting on the floor, looking at the pictures of Sophie. He could write her letters he would never send. Sending them wouldn't be fair. She already had enough to shoulder. She didn't need to read his war experiences as well. He simply couldn't do that to her. But he could try it for himself.

Jonas rose and carried his pad to the desk. He dropped into the chair and pulled out a fresh sheet of paper. *Dear Sophie...*

He wondered how he should begin. At the very beginning or just in the middle? Superficially or down to the smallest detail?

Reluctantly, Jonas retrieved the memories from the depths of his mind and forced himself to return. Back to dust and ashes. To the screams of the dying in his ears. To Philipp's pale face.

Not a single word made it onto the paper.

Instead, Jonas drew deep into the night.

Brisé

Jonas' words buzzed incessantly through her head, as Sophie leaned her forehead against Luca's chest, feeling feverish. She still couldn't believe he had actually left. He had been gone for a week now, and yet every morning, she was disappointed anew that he wasn't home already waiting for her. If her house wasn't still so terribly tidy, there would have been no clue that he had ever been there.

"Hey, Sophie, you're almost asleep," Luca teased, lifting her chin.

The unreal light in his eyes pained her. Despite his closeness, she began to shiver. Ever since the rain, the cold wouldn't let go of her.

Jonas would have put her straight into bed, made her soup and tea, and made sure she rested thoroughly. Luca wanted to dance.

Faintly, Sophie smiled at him. "I'm sorry. My head's just completely stuffed."

"Do you need something to drink?" That was Luca's solution to everything. Everything to keep her dancing with him.

Inevitably, Sophie had to think of Jonas' suspicions that Luca was actually giving her drugs. She shook her head. "Can't we just take a break? I'd really like to get some sleep. This cold has got me pretty bad." Tired, she leaned her forehead back against his chest.

Luca took a step back and looked at her in shock. "Break?" He snorted. "Do you think I ever get a break?"

Her befuddled mind made it hard for Sophie to grasp the meaning of his words.

"All these centuries I've been dancing. Every single night. Don't you think I'd like to take a break, too?" Panic distorted his usually pretty face and made Sophie shudder.

Staggering, she took a step back.

Utterly exhausted, Luca rubbed his hands over his face. "Man, Sophie!" He took her in his arms and whispered placably, "I'm sorry. I didn't mean to snap at you. I've been so terribly nervous lately. I've never been this close. I can already taste freedom on my tongue. To know that this moment is within my grasp... Forgive me, my love!"

All at once, her worries seemed insignificant to her. Of course, it was impossible to interrupt their dance. Not now that they'd come so far. "No, I'm sorry. I was just thinking of myself."

"I need you so much, Sophie," Luca pleaded. "But I don't want you to overextend yourself."

His pitiful tone made Sophie pull herself together and straighten her back. She took Luca's hands, and together they danced across the pond again. Blissfully, he beamed at her.

All her willpower, however, could not banish the headache and fever. "Tomas wouldn't happen to have any tea for a cold?"

Gaining new hope, Luca kissed her hands. "Something much better!" Exuberantly, he spun her around and carried her to their boat. "I'll be right back at your side."

Sophie leaned forward and rested her head on her arms as she watched Luca go. With swift steps, he reached Tomas's bar and interrupted his brother at his work, gesticulating fiercely. Even from here, his concern was abundantly clear, giving Sophie a warm feeling in her stomach. Tomas, however, shook his head before gesturing in her direction. Whatever they were arguing about was slowly beginning to blur with the dull ache in her head. Tired, Sophie closed her eyes.

"You have to leave now." Suddenly, there was someone else in her boat; a young woman with tangled hair. "Now, while his back is turned."

Confused, Sophie looked over at Luca, who had both hands resting on the bar, behind which Tomas had defiantly crossed his arms. "I can't go. Luca needs me."

In a panic, the woman shook her head so that her curls flew into the air. "You have to leave. Now. Soon it will be too late." Before Sophie could respond, the woman had taken her hands in hers and squeezed them so tightly Sophie winced. "Only bad luck awaits you if you stay with him," she implored Sophie urgently. "You must not trust him."

A clearing of the throat made Sophie's seatmate flinch violently. Luca had returned and was frowning at the woman. Immediately, the stranger withdrew. As she hurried away, she kept glancing over her shoulder as if the devil himself were after her.

"Poor thing," Luca muttered and sat down. In his hand, he held a glass that was obviously meant for Sophie. At first glance, the cocktail looked no different from the previous ones, but then she noticed the golden and silver swathes in the blue drink.

"Who was that?"

Luca sighed. "One of the lost souls. She lost her mind after her boyfriend left her. Was a bad story. Now she doesn't trust any man and wants to save her sex from us or something." He shrugged and handed Sophie the cocktail.

Sophie looked once more for the woman, but she had already disappeared into the crowd of hungry creatures. "I feel sorry for her." She looked back at Luca and pulled the glass close. "What's this?"

"Just drink." Gently, Luca guided her hand to her mouth.

It didn't even occur to Sophie to refuse him. She was curious about the new creation. Only Tomas' sombre look with which he watched her from his bar unsettled her, but then the first drops wet her lips and the taste made the world around her blur.

The drink ran down her throat like liquid fire, burning any sickness out of her body. A restlessness took possession of her, reaching all the way to the tips of her toes. Sophie was suddenly so full of energy and drive that she couldn't sit still for a minute longer. She had to dance, had to let the energy out again. And although her head was spinning and she could barely take a straight step, her hands found Luca's and her feet fell in line with his.

His eyes shone like they hadn't in a long time, and Sophie thought he had never looked better. His gaze gave her back all the strength she had lost through the illness, while the alcohol did the rest.

The only thing that could neither be dispelled by Luca's smile or Tomas' magic potion was the cold.

—

The alarm clock had been ringing for five minutes. The penetrating beep entered Sophie's mind, where it intertwined with the eternal melody. She lay motionless in her bed and listened to the discordant sounds. Thought only detached itself gradually from the viscous mass of her sleepy mind, even though she had to get up and get ready so that she wouldn't be late.

For half an eternity, she waited for Jonas to bang on her door and force her to leave the bed. But he didn't come. Like the weeks before, the flat remained silent, apart from her alarm clock. No rattling of drawers, no hissing in the pan, and no rustling of bags.

Tears made their way across her face and slowly rolled into her hair and onto the pillow beneath her. Panting, Sophie wiped the corners of her eyes and sat up. Her head was pounding, which wasn't entirely due to the alarm clock she finally turned off. Listlessly, she looked around her room, unable to decide on any of her clothes. Finally, she reached for the nearest one, sniffed it briefly, and decided it would do. With a few moves, she had tied her hair up and left the room.

For a while, Sophie had tried to keep Jonas's precious order, but now, the guest house had returned to its former state. She finally found her shoes on the sofa where she had angrily thrown them that morning.

Sophie didn't know why she had been so terribly angry, only that the magic of The DeModie had vanished all of a sudden, and she had been alone. She didn't even have Jonas's phone number. Her father had to have it—after all, he had hired him—but so far, she hadn't managed to ask him for it. After all, it was her fault Jonas had left. Not that he'd told her father that. As far as she knew, he hadn't even mentioned Sophie when he'd handed in his notice.

That was just like him, she thought as she tipped yoghurt over her cereal. He would rather put up with being seen as unreliable as to rat her out to her father. It only made the words he had thrown into her face worse.

The initial defiance had quickly faded after the cold robbed her of all strength. Instead, she'd recognised the shred of truth in his statements and wished she could turn back time.

In contrast to the taste explosion of Tomas' mixed drinks, her muesli tasted bland. In general, there was nothing outside The DeModie that excited Sophie anymore. She hardly even noticed the green buds outside her window, which had always brought a smile to her lips in the past. Everything had blurred into a colourless grey.

In two months, the year and the last day were over, and Sophie felt like she was facing a big fat nothing. She had missed all the dance dates and didn't believe she could ever pull off such a performance again. Then she had nothing. No training, no education, no future. Worst of all, she couldn't even muster enough energy to care anymore.

~

Luca had long since ceased to be the radiant prince he had always been for Sophie. Night after night, they danced, and yet, they grew more and more distant from each other. As the weeks passed, Sophie realised how little she actually had in common with the handsome prince. Jonas had been right. Luca never asked how she was or took an interest in her worries and hopes. Yet he must have noticed that her body and mental health were deteriorating.

Sophie had always fancied that he loved dancing as much as she did, but Luca's eyes remained cold when the music sounded. He led her and let her shine: technically correct, but without any passion. For him, dancing was just a duty, the necessary evil to escape the curse. Even Frederick had been more in love with the music.

Luca shared neither her ambitions nor her dreams. All he wanted was freedom, and Sophie couldn't blame him. She still felt sorry for him and his brothers, and wished she could release them all. But more than that, she longed for the year to end.

"What do you want to do first when you get out?" asked Sophie, when the evening was still relatively young, and her senses were not yet as befuddled by the music and usual mix of cocktails. Late at night, time at The DeModie always blurred into one wild dance, of which she barely kept any memories.

Luca shrugged. "Whatever you want to do."

Sighing, Sophie turned into his arm. She had hoped she wouldn't also have to play tour guide when the time came. "I'll probably sleep for a month."

With a hearty chuckle, Luca put his arms around her. "Should I ask Tomas for another drink?"

"Later," she said, shaking her head. "What's going to happen to your brothers when you're free, anyway?" Sophie snuggled back against his chest, but something didn't feel right. They were the wrong arms holding her.

Luca's hot breath brushed the back of her neck and a comforting shiver ran down Sophie's spine. "They'll have to find their own dancers. Jasper seems to be doing quite well at the moment."

He nodded further forward, and Sophie saw the younger brother flirting with three young girls who burst into giggles at almost every word he said. Almost casually, he stroked the arm of one, who blatantly adored him for it. It had been less than a year since Sophie had hung on Luca's lips in the very same way, while her friends had the time of their lives.

She missed Pia and the others. Those early days at The DeModie, when they still came here together every day, had been the best summer of their lives. At first, they had to persuade Sophie to finally go partying again, but soon it was she who had urged the others to return to the strange dance club. Now she was the only one who still came. Her friends had long since moved on.

She sighed heavily and turned to Luca. As usual, he didn't ask what was bothering her. He was content as long as she was spinning in circles. As soon as she tired, he called for Tomas, and Sophie lost herself again in the tangled downward spiral of The DeModie.

***

The days grew noticeably longer again, and the cold weather finally gave way to spring. All at once, the trees turned green, and people ventured outdoors again. The cocktail that Luca gave Sophie to get her through the night often led to a restlessness that kept her still wandering aimlessly in the morning, instead of giving her body a chance to recover. In the process, the melody of The DeModie haunted her into the day.

For hours, Sophie roamed around the park after her night of dancing, watching the people who had it all figured out: the businessmen whose ears were always glued to the phone; the teenagers who gathered in the secluded corners of the park; the students who took advantage of the spring weather to lie in the grass under the sun and study. They all lived by day, had goals and dreams they were pursuing. They were free.

When she walked like this, her thoughts jumped from Luca to Jonas and back again. The one who wouldn't let her go and the other who had abandoned her. Instead of gaining a prince, she had lost a friend, and with him, all hope.

Her smartphone vibrated in her pocket and jolted Sophie from her mental carousel. An event invitation from Pia. She didn't even need to look it up to know she couldn't make it. Despite that, she longed for time with her friends.

Even though she knew that all she had to do was call them to meet for coffee, she couldn't bring herself to do it. It had been too long since she had heard from either, and too long since she had experienced anything that wasn't tied to Luca. Each of her days was like the one before.

The display showed three missed calls, and for a moment, her heartbeat quickened. But the calls weren't from Jonas, only her father. He had even left a voicemail. Sophie had heard it ringing so many times, but she'd always lacked the strength to answer the calls.

Instead, she listened to the voicemail. "Hey, kiddo." By now, he had reverted to her old nickname, a sign of his increasing perplexity. "I was hoping you'd call back sometime, but I'm probably only annoying you with these calls. I just want to know how you are. I miss you, Sophie. Maybe you can find some time to write me a message or just come over. Anything." A long silence followed, but he hadn't hung up, perhaps hoping she'd pick up after all. "My door is always open," he began again, his voice sounding strangely choked. "You know that, right? Whatever you need, I'm here for you."

Sophie listened to the message three more times, just to hear his voice. Despite his words, she felt so terribly alone. Like the cold, the loneliness had never gone away.

Jonas had often told her that it was she who kept him alive, who had been a light in his darkness. Yet she hadn't noticed how he had become her lighthouse until he was gone. Now that she was alone, she missed him more than anything.

Slowly, the effect of the mixture wore off, and Sophie sank onto a park bench, relieved to rest her feet. As long as the music and stimulant were still coursing through her body, she never managed to keep her feet still. Instead, she always had to run, always had to dance.

Sophie took out the little music box Jonas had given her for Christmas. As she watched the ballerina spin incessantly on one standing leg, her heart contracted. Despite the terrible panic attacks, Jonas had been far too good for her. He had cared for her when she hadn't been able to, had spoiled her with attention, and never asked for more than to be allowed to stay near her. And she had shamelessly taken advantage of him.

She wondered if he was all right. Sophie thought of his terrible nightmares and had to shudder. Every time they hit him, he'd been a mess, and after New Year's Eve, it had only gotten worse. She'd noticed how he'd tried to drown his fears in alcohol, and now the guilt gnawed at her that she'd let it happen.

Jonas had always been content with what little she had given him. Yet she should have done so much more. Should have dragged him to the doctor and thrown out all the alcohol. But she hadn't had the energy, had been too lost herself.

"Look, Mum, a ballerina!" The child's bright voice made Sophie jump up. Startled, she looked at the little girl pointing at her mother's hand. At her and not the music box. Because she was wearing tattered pointe shoes and a tulle skirt that billowed around her hips.

The mother's gaze was less benevolent, probably because her night of drinking was clearly written on her face. Gently, she pulled the girl aside and spoke to her. Sophie couldn't hear the words, but the tone was weirdly familiar. Her mother's voice had had a similar warm sound.

Suddenly swallowing, Sophie averted her eyes. Between the trees, she could spot a playground with children playing under the watchful gaze of their parents. Two young mothers pushed their prams past her as they chatted about their offspring's latest progress. Their eyes shone with pride, just as her mother's had done when she danced her first steps on the dance floor.

Sophie saw them clearly in front of her. Her dark eyes had gleamed in joyful anticipation even before Sophie had taken the stage. That day, Sophie had danced only for her, missing all the cues. Years later, she had been more focused, but when she was nervous, she only had to look left to the second row and find her calm in the confident glow of her mother.

It had been Sophie's second performance in the municipal theatre when her mother's proud look had suddenly turned to nothing. The instruments in her solo had dropped out one by one and a restlessness had gripped the auditorium. No one had thought of her while helpers, onlookers, and finally the paramedics had gathered around her mother and begun resuscitation efforts. After a while, Sophie had noticed the gentle pressure around her wrist. Someone had been talking to her, but none of the words had got through. At last, she'd followed her dance teacher down from the stage and towards the cluster of people. In the eyes of those who let her pass, she read what she'd already known.

It had been a walk Sophie had never been able to reverse. She hadn't stepped on stage since.

Completely out of breath, Sophie reached the cemetery where her mother had been put to rest. Her head was spinning with the dizziness that so often followed her exhaustion. Cursing, she stumbled around among the graves, trying to remember the day when she and her father had buried her mother. The memories were blurred, as if the day's haze of tears still hung over them. The painful pounding in her head did little to help her remember.

Frustrated and desperate, Sophie stopped and looked around. Why hadn't she come here before? What kind of daughter didn't visit her mother's grave in two and a half years? A young pear tree caught her eye, and the memory came back.

Her mother had loved pears and wished to be buried under such a tree.

This early in the year, it was covered all over with delicate white blossoms. A breeze brushed through the branches and a shower of petals trickled down onto the grave between its roots. Sophie's knees gave way, and she sank to the ground, gasping. Hot tears ran down her cheeks and breathing became immeasurably more difficult.

"I messed up," she confessed between sobs that shook her whole body. "Mum, I completely messed up. Jonas is gone!" Startled, Sophie covered her mouth, surprised by her own vehemence. "They're all gone, and I'm so alone!"

Howling, Sophie collapsed on the grave, not caring that grass and dirt soon ruined her tulle dress. Her fingers dug into the soft earth as long-pent-up anger seized her. "How could you do this to me? Just like that? People don't die at thirty-eight! And especially not during my performance. Why didn't you tell me the doctor had put you on bed rest? You could have seen me some other time."

Her tears kept flowing incessantly, and for several minutes, Sophie was shaken so violently by cramps that she even threw up bile and little else. Suddenly, she was overcome by all the feelings she had suppressed for years. There was anger and rage at the mother who had left her alone, deep sorrow for the only person who had shared her passion for dancing, and pain tied to the loss of her best friend in this world. On top of all this, guilt hovered like the Sword of Damocles, threatening to pierce Sophie. How many times had she argued with her mother?

Threatened to quit ballet just because she knew it would hurt her more than anything else? She had been offended so many times when her mother had failed to accompany her. So many angry words had been spoken that she could never take back.

"I'm so sorry. I'm so terribly sorry for everything" Sophie choked the words from her throat. "I didn't mean for this to happen. It's all my fault!" Just before the performance, they had been shouting at each other because she had stayed up too late drinking.

"Can't you take dancing seriously for once? God, Sophie! I don't understand you. You're so talented and still you pull all this shit." They were in the dressing room where her mother was vigorously tying her hair in a bun. The knot was too tight, and Sophie cried out indignantly.

"You're hurting me," she complained and raised a hand.

Her mother slapped her hand away and straightened the bun.

"The others were celebrating, too."

In the mirror, her mother's eyes glared at her. "But you're not like the others. Your body is your asset. If you want to make it in the dance world, you can't go out partying and getting drunk until the wee hours." She held her hand over her mouth and coughed.

"What if I don't want to make it?" Sophie crossed her arms. "Maybe being on stage isn't my big dream, after all."

Her mother rolled her eyes and pulled her to her feet, regardless of her protest. "I don't have time for your childish behaviour right now. We have to go."

"I'm not being childish! I just want to have fun for once," Sophie scoffed, stamping her foot defiantly. *"And maybe have a life and not just fulfil your dream because you can't do it anymore. I'm not your puppet."*

In exasperation, her mother let go of Sophie. "Go ahead! Throw away everything you've worked for! Abandon your company and ruin your body with alcohol!"

In the end, Sophie had followed obediently. In the car, they had still maintained an offended silence, but at the theatre, her mother had hugged her as usual and kissed her on the forehead before putting on the shoes Sophie was allowed to wear for these performances. The shoes her mother had worn as Sleeping Beauty before she had to give up professional dancing.

They were the same shoes that were on her battered feet now. The shoes Sophie could no longer take off, no matter how tattered they were. In the end, she had got her way. Instead of dancing on stage, she had gone to parties and enjoyed life to the fullest.

Now she was terribly ashamed of it. "I just couldn't go back without you watching me. You weren't there anymore, and who else was I going to dance for?"

Jonas came to her mind. In his gaze, she had felt safe again, had felt the recognition and excitement that ballet brought her. And how had Sophie thanked him? By pushing him away, just like her mother, and saying the worst things she had found inside her. Just so that she wouldn't have to look at herself in the mirror.

She missed him so much.

"Luca! I never got to tell you about Luca. He needs me so much and loves me. You would have liked him." No, she wouldn't. On the contrary, her mother would have been horrified to learn that she had jeopardised her career and thrown away her talent for a boy. And Sophie would have screamed at her with indignation that it was entirely her decision. "I think I might have made a mistake."

Blinking, Sophie looked at the grave as the full brunt of the truth hit her. "I shouldn't have given it up. You always said to keep at it and that I had so much talent. Jonas said the same thing. He was my second chance, but I drove him away. Just like you, Mum." Again, spasms shook her as she thought back to Jonas' disappointed face in the rain. He had begged so many times, even pleaded with her, but she hadn't wanted to hear what he had to say because Luca's light had blinded her too much. Luca, who was both her curse and the fulfilment of all her desires.

"I can't dance anymore. I don't want to," Sophie sobbed. "Everything hurts and I hate it. You're not here and Jonas isn't here. I can't even talk to Dad because he would be utterly disappointed. I miss you so much, Mum." Crying, she rested her forehead on the cool earth. "And I'm so terribly tired."

—

Startled, Sophie jerked up when the sun was already glowing red on the horizon. In her exhaustion, she had fallen asleep in her dirty clothes on top of the grave. Confused, Sophie blinked up at the evening sun and wiped her sticky cheeks before realising how dirty her hands were. Only then did she realise that she only had a few minutes before she had to be back at The DeModie.

"I have to go, Mum. But I'll be back. I will," she cried as she flew away in her shoes.

There was no time to return home and make herself look pretty. Her heart raced as she imagined Luca's disappointment. He had been stood up once before, and Sophie had sworn she would never do that to him.

When she reached the Niemeyer Street, darkness was falling.

"There you are," Tomas said, throwing the door wide open. "Luca's already freaking out."

No question how she was. No interest in the fact that she looked like she'd just risen from the grave. Earth hung in clumps in her hair and dirt covered her cheeks. Her eyes were badly reddened, her make-up smeared. The dress was rumpled and covered in dirt, but Tomas didn't say a word, merely closed the door behind him. It felt like he was taking her breath away with it.

Hastily, Sophie hurried down the stairs through the wondrous forest, which had long since lost all beauty for her. At the bottom, Luca waited for her. He exhaled audibly as she threw herself from the last steps directly into his arms. Before she could even explain to him what had delayed her, the music started playing and Luca swept her away into the dance.

Sophie stumbled after him and let herself be led. It took several minutes before she had enough breath to speak. Not once, however, did Luca inquire about her condition. They danced as if it was the most ordinary thing in the world that she looked more like a homeless person than a princess.

"I need to talk to you," Sophie finally managed to say, slowly stringing the words in her head together.

Alarmed, Luca's eyes widened. "Do you need a drink?"

"No!" Sophie objected vehemently, tempted to punch him in the arm. "I want to talk to you about our future." She needed a plan, some glimmer of light that promised her new hope. In the past, he had promised to lay the world at her feet, but now she needed concrete arrangements. She needed to know that all was not lost yet.

Luca's grip became immeasurably stronger, causing Sophie to wince. "You're not going to abandon me now, are you?" With some effort, Sophie managed to shake her head. "We're so close, Sophie. I'll give you everything you need. Treasures, magic, means to carry you through the night. Everything."

Startled, Sophie stared at him. She had never seen him so manic. "You're hurting me!" His fingers were digging painfully into her skin.

"Promise me you won't leave me hanging now!" Luca pleaded.

Disappointed, Sophie nodded her head. She no longer had the strength to argue with him. "I promise, yes." Luca's face relaxed immediately, and they danced on as if nothing had ever happened, as if she wasn't on the verge of a breakdown.

There was nothing more Sophie could say or do. Even if she had been able to bring herself to abandon him, her shoes would have carried her back to The DeModie again and again.

Relevé

The countryside rushed past Jonas' train window while he was deep in thought. Flowering meadows, glittering rivers, and dark forests. A bird of prey circled high in the air, and in the paddocks horses stood with their foals. Life was blossoming around him.

Only twenty more minutes and the train would arrive in Sophie's hometown. The prospect gave him a queasy feeling, while also filling him with joyous anticipation. He had missed her—his ballerina—although it had been the right decision to leave. He had needed help, just as Sophie had said, and he had finally got it.

Sometimes, when melancholy gripped him, Jonas thought that he might not even be alive without her. He wouldn't have possessed the will to face his memories, nor would he have found his way out. He owed Sophie so much, first and foremost an apology. That was why he was now sitting on the train, eagerly awaiting their reunion.

The train came to a screeching halt in the station. The small jolt, while Jonas was already standing in the doorway, made him flinch for a moment. Yet it was only the train's brake, nothing sinister. Taking a deep breath, Jonas exited the train, his bag slung over one shoulder.

Once he was on the platform, he waited until the crowd had dispersed and he could breathe again. During that, the little shop in the station caught his eye, and without further ado, Jonas decided to buy a bunch of flowers for Sophie. Then he made his way home.

With every step, his anxiety grew. What if she didn't want to see him after the argument? Maybe Jonas should have called after all or sent one of the letters he had never written. But he just had to see Sophie. Had to know that it had all been worth it.

Therapy had been hell. Jonas remembered the countless days on the edge with a shudder as he finally turned onto the road to the Kallenbach estate. For a brief moment, the familiar sight made his knees weak. Almost hesitantly, he stepped up to the threshold and knocked loudly. No answer. A second time he knocked, but nothing moved behind the door. For a moment, he wondered if Sophie might be out, but it was late in the morning and bright daylight, and therefore the time when she would be at home. He knocked again, then noticed that the door wasn't latched. When he peered in cautiously, Jonas almost dropped his bag in shock.

Sophie had never been particularly tidy, but he hadn't expected such a mess. As if in a trance, he stepped into the flat and hardly recognised it. The floor was covered with dirty laundry and dirty dishes. Fruit flies swarmed around a half-filled smoothie cup, whose colour had turned bluish-grey. Then a corrosive stench crept into Jonas' nose. Disgusted, he looked around and spotted the vomit next to the sofa.

"Sophie?" he called into the room, but received no reply. Judging by the furry coating on the dishes, they hadn't been touched in weeks.

Without further ado, Jonas put down his bag, grabbed a rubbish bag and began to clean up the mess. He took three rubbish bags outside before collecting the laundry and putting on the first load. Next came the dishes, and finally he set about cleaning up the traces of vomit. The work was good for his head and prevented him from thinking too much about how it could have come this far, or possibly blaming himself for it. Energetically, Jonas tore open the windows in the hope of finally getting rid of the stench, and discovered more rubbish the next moment. It took hours to get the flat back to shape.

"Jonas?" Sophie stood at the threshold of her bedroom, leaning heavily against the doorframe.

His eyes widened when he saw her standing there. *So fragile*, flashed through his mind. In a flash, he was with her, holding her tightly against him. In his arms, he felt her much too thin body trembling. "What's wrong, Sophie?"

"I'm so cold," Sophie replied, completely out of it.

Jonas held her at a distance to regard her more closely and noticed that Sophie didn't manage to look him in the eye. Instead, her gaze wandered unsteadily, never lingering on one point long enough. Her eyes were red, deep shadows beneath them. Her hair was stringy and unkempt, her skin pale and sunken. She looked more dead than alive. No wonder she was cold.

Inevitably, he lowered his gaze until he saw the shoes, which were little more than rags of cloth, dirty and frayed. Through the thinned leather, he could see the bruises and scraped areas. Rusty brown stains stood out from under the dirt. "Damn it, Sophie!" muttered Jonas, pulling her close to him again.

For minutes, he held her close until her trembling finally subsided. Instead, she swayed dangerously in his arms. Jonas picked her up and carried her over to the sofa before bringing in countless blankets to wrap her in. "You'd best get some more sleep while I do the shopping, go to the pharmacy, and make you something decent to eat." He knew she'd only just got out of bed, but judging by the bags under her eyes, she was in dire need of more sleep. "I'll be right back." Sophie nodded weakly and was asleep mere seconds later.

Jonas turned away and left the flat. For a moment, he considered calling an ambulance, but then remembered what had happened the last time he had interfered in her life. Sophie didn't seem to be in acute danger of dying, despite her condition. He should at least talk to her first before deciding something over her head again. Besides, the emergency doctor would probably want to keep her there overnight, and Sophie wouldn't like that at all.

Jonas set about making Sophie a fortifying potato soup and brewing tea. While the potatoes were boiling, he sat down on the back of the sofa and carefully untied the laces of her shoes. Just the sight of her feet hurt him. He lovingly stroked the battered toes and then bent down for the flannel. He carefully wet the encrusted dirt with warm water, but still Sophie shot up, hissing. Her fingers tightened on the back of the sofa, and she pressed her lips together to stifle a moan.

Her eyes glistened suspiciously. Then she blinked and brought her hand to her mouth, startled. "You really came back."

Jonas nodded as he carefully brushed the dirt off her feet. "Indeed. I did."

With a towel, he dabbed at her feet as gently as he could, but Sophie still dropped back onto the couch, panting. "They hurt so much," she whined.

Guilt tugged at Jonas' chest. He applied the cream he had bought at the pharmacy and finally stood up. "I'll get the tea ready for you."

Sophie just sighed weakly, one hand on her forehead, and her eyes fixed on the ceiling.

Concerned, Jonas poured the hot water before turning his attention briefly to the soup and mashing the potatoes. The silence almost hurt him physically, and he knew he had to dispel it. Silence was never good.

"I was in town and thought I'd stop by." With a wry grin, he looked over at her and was pleased that she returned his gaze, even if her eyes were strangely vacant. "That's bullshit, of course," Jonas admitted. "I'm here because of you. After all that, I had to see you again."

He turned down the hot plate and brought her the warm tea. "You really can't be left alone either." As Sophie took the cup in her bony fingers, Jonas stroked her hair lovingly.

"I didn't have time to clean up. If I'd known you were coming..." she began and faltered, as if she'd just realised she didn't have to pretend. She lowered her eyes. "I thought you were still mad at me."

Surprised, Jonas stared at her. "Mad? Sophie, I was never mad at you. Alright, maybe a little, but the problem wasn't you; it was me. How could I presume to give you advice, or rather throw it into your face, when I was standing on the edge myself? No, I was more angry at myself for not being able to help you."

Tentatively, a smile came to her lips, as if she didn't quite dare be happy about it. Again, Jonas got up and returned to the stove. "By the way, I returned home and started therapy. The beginning was pretty rough. I almost gave up, but now it's slowly getting better. I'm learning to cope with the triggers and sort of get over what I experienced."

The memories of therapy sessions were hardly better than those of the war, but his therapist had been right. With time, the visions lost their horror. "There's still a long way to go, but at least I can see an end now. I even enrolled at uni last month." Smiling, he glanced at her to make sure she was drinking the tea. Sophie, however, seemed enthralled by his words. "Engineering. It's where I'll learn how to build things instead of breaking them."

The little joke elicited a chuckle, and her eyes lit up briefly. The sound was only a faint echo of the laughter that had caught his attention. But it brought some colour back to her cheeks, and her gaze was no longer quite so blank.

"Yes, I've reconsidered the architecture thing. It would've been great, but I think I need something tangible first. Besides, I don't have the nerve to put together an elaborate application portfolio just yet. Maybe I'll try my luck after my bachelor's degree. Although I have to say that I really like engineering. I didn't realise how much I missed maths and physics."

Sophie widened her eyes in disbelief. "Maths and physics? One can miss that?"

"Yes, now I can once more." Thoughtfully, Jonas filled a deep plate with the hearty soup and placed it on the table.

Sophie eyed the food with almost reverential respect. She swallowed, and for a moment, Jonas feared she would refuse. But then she sat up and carefully began to spoon up the soup.

"It's also not so much the mathematics itself, but rather the feeling that everything has an inert logic. There are rules and laws, and if you follow them, you get something solid. It's a wonderful feeling."

"You certainly seem better," Sophie remarked between spoonfuls. "Aren't you eating?"

It would've been enough for him to watch her do it, but for solidarity's sake, Jonas got up to fetch himself a plate. Sitting down again, Jonas finally dared to ask the question that was burning on his tongue. "And you? How are you?" Her spoon paused in mid-air. "Are you still dancing with your prince?"

Sophie's spoon dropped back into the soup as she stared at him like a deer in headlights.

Jonas regretted asking, but he had to know the answer.

Eventually, Sophie's stupor dissolved, and she nodded slightly. "Yes, six more days." All at once, her eyes filled with tears, and she desperately blinked to keep from crying.

"Sophie, what's wrong?" Jonas asked anxiously, leaning over the table to take her left hand in his and squeeze it tightly.

In annoyance, Sophie wiped the tears from the corners of her eyes. "This is so ridiculous. You're finally getting better, and here I am, bringing all my problems to you."

Immediately, Jonas reassured her, "Hey, that's why I'm here. I care about you, and I want to know how you're doing."

"Horribly?" Sophie said with a helpless shrug. "You see. I'm a wreck, a total failure. You've tried to talk sense into me so many times, and what have I done? Drank and danced." She had to catch her breath for a moment before she could continue, "You've been so good to me, and I've been mooning over my stupid prince."

The memory still hurt, but the words also gave him unexpected hope. Cautiously, Jonas inquired, "Stupid prince?"

"He doesn't care about me in the slightest," Sophie suddenly became exasperated, regaining some of her fire. "It's all about him, all the time. I mean, I get that the curse sucks, but I'm in it, too. I'm keeping my promise. Is it too much to ask that I have a good cry on his shoulder once in a while?"

Startled, she looked at Jonas, and all at once, the tears fell. "He never listens to me, and he doesn't care whether I look pretty or run down. I could come down the stairs bleeding, and he'd just sweep me off into a dance. I don't know how I could ever fall in love with such a narcissistic egomaniac. I feel like I'm just a means to an end for him. Interchangeable."

The words echoed all the prejudices and worries Jonas had always held in regard to Luca. "But you still go every night?"

Sophie nodded. "Well, it's almost over now." She looked thoughtfully at the table before looking up with a sudden determination. "But then I'm breaking up with him. As soon as we're out, I never want to have anything to do with him again."

Jonas' heart skipped a beat before it thumped in excitement. That Sophie would end her unhealthy relationship with Luca was more than he could have dreamed of. He wanted to tell her how he felt about her at that moment, but he knew it wasn't the right time. She'd just decided to break up with the love of her life. She definitely wouldn't have any interest in a new relationship. This was about her and not him. So Jonas kept silent and enjoyed her eating the soup.

"It tastes really delicious," Sophie finally said, with a smile that warmed his heart. "Thank you for coming back, Jonas. I missed you."

Jonas looked after Sophie for the rest of the week and accompanied her back to The DeModie at her request. Although he had the coat with him, he dared no further intrusion on his own, and Sophie never asked him to. She recovered a little under his care, but her apathy and low resilience worried him increasingly, and he feverishly awaited the day when this business with Luca would finally be over.

His anger at Luca for pushing her so far kept smouldering under the surface, but Jonas kept his mouth shut and didn't allow himself to make a derogatory remark. Sophie seemed to have noticed on her own that her Prince Charming was a true nightmare instead.

"You can do it." He built her up on the eve of the last dance. The sun hadn't set yet, and the clubs were closed. Still, the unobtrusive door between the two large dance bars would soon swing open.

Lost in thought, Sophie looked at her feet. "Yeah, I guess I will." He knew that despite what she was about to do, it wouldn't be easy for her to give up Luca.

Once more, Jonas took her in his arms and squeezed her. "It's just this night. You dance with Luca one more time and then never again. I promise you, everything will be better from tomorrow on."

Her eyes were misty as she looked up at him and tried to smile. Sophie didn't quite manage it, but he could see the glow in her eyes he had missed so much. With a grimace of distress, she finally walked towards The DeModie. As if by magic, the door opened, and shortly afterwards, the mysterious club had swallowed Sophie up again.

Sighing, Jonas turned around and decided to stretch his legs a little more. He already knew that this night would be interminably long. Sleeping was out of the question today.

His feet carried him through the streets, which were quite busy on this spring evening. In a small studio, through the large windows, he saw a group of young dancers doing their ballet exercises. For a moment, Jonas stopped and watched them. Amazed at himself, he could name all their positions. He even noticed the little posture mistakes that some of them made now and then.

Once, Sophie had also danced in such a studio, concentrating intently, her toes stretched high above her head. She had laughed with the others and let herself fall into the music. He clearly saw her in front of him as she had appeared to him on his first day: full of life and with an unparalleled elegance.

Before someone could shoo him away, Jonas set off again, bought himself something to eat and began to wander aimlessly. If he couldn't sleep, he would have been better off using the time to catch up on his lectures, but the thought of Sophie and her ordeal wouldn't let him go. Inevitably, his feet led him back to the vicinity of the club.

Other revellers had arrived, but the door of The DeModie remained closed. For a moment, Jonas thought about staying out all night, then he tore himself away from the sight and walked away. Sophie would reproach him if he acted this controlling. And rightfully so.

Lost in thought, he almost tripped over the beggar who was squeezing into the darkness of a side street. Jonas wanted to go on, but then he looked into the man's bright blue eyes and realised with surprise that it was the same man who had given him the coat almost a year ago. He'd also recognised Jonas and patted the ground enthusiastically beside him.

With a smile, Jonas sat down and promptly handed him his leftover cheeseburger. Greedily, the man began to eat and remarked with his mouth full, "You don't look rich but happy. Guess you didn't go in, after all."

"Because there's no way The DeModie can make you happy?" asked Jonas with a grin, knowing his own answer to that. "I was inside, twice, but I didn't recover my treasure."

Thoughtfully, the beggar gave him the once-over, then wiped his mouth and the sauce in his beard. Wearily, Jonas handed him a handkerchief, whereupon the blue eyes twinkled with amusement. "You should have taken gold and silver. The rest isn't worth it."

"It's not?" Jonas echoed, a maddening thought occurring to him. "What's your business with The DeModie, anyway? You don't seem to be tied to it."

The beggar laughed hoarsely. "Not anymore."

Jonas buzzed with excitement. The answer he sought was just beyond his reach. "Not anymore? Then you were once one of them. How did you..." There was the answer, incredulous as it might seem. "You're one of the princes."

"Seems like you've been studying up on The DeModie," the beggar replied appreciatively, and immediately sat up much straighter. Still, he and Luca were worlds apart. The beggar seemed to have the same thought, for he snorted, "Yes, you don't see much of it anymore. The magic fades. This world is ruining it. It breaks us all, but most of all, it holds no magic, preserves no illusions."

A deep sadness took hold of Jonas as he pondered the truth of his words. The world was indeed a dark place. "But not always," he objected nonetheless. "There is some magic." He couldn't help thinking of Sophie's beautiful smile. "The magic of music. The magic of laughter."

The former prince looked at him wistfully. "It still exists, but finding it..." He looked into the distance. "I had it once. All the happiness in the world was in my hands and I sold it." When Jonas looked at him questioningly, the beggar sighed. "Sina. My girl. For a year, she danced with me, laughed with me, told me about all the wonders of the upper world." Again, he sighed and sank into the memories. "I can still see her, but she doesn't laugh anymore."

Restlessly, Jonas shifted in his seat. He hadn't given a thought to the girl who must have freed the man beside him. Sophie's predecessor. He wondered if Luca loved Sophie as much as his brother had his dancer. And now she wanted to leave him.

Finally, he got up the nerve to ask, "What happened to her?"

The beggar collapsed under the weight of his guilt. "What happened? She's taken my place. That's the way the curse works." The blue eyes pleaded for forgiveness. The beggar's hands began to tremble and tears ran down his cheeks.

Jonas stared at the man as the terrible meaning of it all dawned on him. He jumped up and started running. He ran like he had never run before in his life. Ran until his lungs burned. All in the wild hope that it wasn't too late yet.

Coda

Hundreds of eyes stared at Sophie as she glided across the castle square into Luca's arms. The dark battlements towered menacingly above her, but the hungry eyes in the countless faces around her were worse. None bore any resemblance to the people she had met before. Instead, furry, clawed, sharp-toothed monsters glared at her. Every nightmare she'd ever had seemed to be represented, and they were all just waiting to tear her to shreds.

Safety was only found in Luca's face, for he was as radiant as he'd been on the first day. He cared for her, joked and laughed, and was quite the perfect prince tonight. Maybe everything would work out after all, if only they could finally get out of here.

Sophie had to stop herself from constantly looking at the clock. Here, in The DeModie, it was always night and there were always clouds in the sky. Luca's excitement filled her as well, and yet failed to carry her away. She smiled, but her heart was no longer in it. It took too much energy to set her feet and keep her composure. How tired she was of the music here now.

"You look beautiful today," Luca cooed as he arched her back and gently brushed his lips across her neck. Her hand came to rest on the back of his neck and held onto it as he pulled her back up.

Sophie had dolled herself up for the last evening. Her hair was braided and the dress provocative as ever. Her make-up hid the traces of fatigue and alcohol, and even without the cocktail, she'd managed to put on her best performance tonight. Only her mother's shoes didn't quite fit with everything. Maybe it was time to hang them up.

With a shudder, Sophie thought of the wall of shoes Jonas had once told her about. Did it really exist, with a hook waiting for her?

Worry crept into Luca's face, for which she was infinitely more grateful than all his compliments. "Is anything amiss?"

"I just need to rest," she replied, gently stroking his cheek before turning under his arm.

Luca awaited her return with a smile. "You shall have that. After tonight, you will get all the rest you deserve." When he kissed Sophie, he stirred the old feelings she had harboured for him for so long. Perhaps she should reconsider her decision to break up with him. After all, she wasn't the only one who had been affected by the year.

Suddenly, however, Luca's gaze drifted away from her, and he frowned. Irritated, Sophie threw a glance over her shoulder and noticed the crowd growing restless and turning away from her. Loud hisses and snarls rang out, and all of a sudden, she could hear Tomas' angry voice.

"You don't belong here," he shouted, yet he couldn't stop the crowd from parting.

Sophie's eyes widened in surprise when she recognised Jonas. Around his shoulders, he wore a shimmering cloak that made him seem almost regal himself. It did not make him invisible, as he had described it to her, but it kept the monsters and Tomas, who was coming after him, at a distance.

When Tomas looked at Luca, his anger immediately turned to submissiveness. "He got it from Immanuel."

Luca's grip on her hand suddenly tightened. His other arm wrapped around her waist and pulled her closer. The hairs on her arms stood up, and all at once, Sophie felt uncomfortable. Jonas' scowl was directed at Luca, but when he came to stand in front of them, it was her he was looking at.

Nervously, Sophie tried to lighten the tense situation, but the words rolled off her tongue with difficulty, "What are you doing here this early?"

"You know him?" Luca asked sharply, before Jonas could answer her. Of course, she had never said a word about Jonas.

"We're going home now, Sophie," Jonas announced in a firm voice. Behind him, Tomas looked as if he wanted to throw him out on the streets, but the coat still instilled respect.

His answer unsettled Sophie, just as Luca's firm grip around her body did. "But the sun is still a long way from rising. You know the curse won't be lifted until dawn." She turned to

Luca. "Jonas is a friend. The best friend I have." Tentatively, she smiled at Jonas, and his features softened a little, while Luca's darkened.

"Fine, then he should wait outside," Luca said, with more than enough bite. "She doesn't need a friend now. Sophie has me." Demonstratively, Luca put a hand under Sophie's chin and turned her face towards him so he could kiss her.

For the first time, the kiss made her uncomfortable, and she squirmed out of his grip. "Don't do that!"

Luca raised an eyebrow and frowned. His look sent an icy chill down Sophie's spine. Determined, she turned away from him.

Jonas had clenched his hands into fists and was staring at the floor. So that was what Luca had intended. Almost gently, her prince repeated, "Sophie is mine."

Indignantly, Sophie wanted to protest, but at that moment, Jonas tore his gaze off the floor. With a glare, he fixed Luca. "Sophie is not a possession! If you loved her, you'd know that."

In a cold voice Sophie had never heard before, Luca mocked Jonas, "Like you do?"

Trembling, Jonas averted his eyes.

A warm feeling spread through her stomach, and her head swam. Jonas had come for her. Now, however, he seemed to lose heart. "Jonas," she whispered, and his head jerked around. "Why are you here?"

Instead of her, he fixed Luca with a stare. Every muscle in his body seemed to be taut. "I love her, yes. I've loved her ever since I first saw her stagger out of this damn club." The warmth inside her spread wider and wider, and when Jonas looked at her, her heart skipped a beat. "Sophie, your laughter enchanted me. It's given me a reason to hope again," he continued. "Without you, I wouldn't be standing here today. I would never have found the courage to face my nightmares. I know you don't like to hear it, but you mean everything to me."

Luca's grip around her waist began to hurt. Jonas' words, on the other hand, had released something beautiful in Sophie, something she hadn't been aware of before. Luca's light had burned everything else that remained of her life. But now, her fingertips tingled, and the corners of her mouth twitched irretrievably upwards.

All the little things that connected her to Jonas replayed in her mind. The way he'd looked at her when he thought she didn't know. The way he'd watched over her, even when she'd acted like the biggest brat in the world. The devotion with which he had rooted for her and with which he had held up her dreams and rebuilt them for her. Jonas knew her like no one else. From day one, he had seen straight behind her façade, made her pain his, and tried to fix what she'd refused to even acknowledge.

"How touching," Luca said, his voice tense. "But she's with me. Isn't that right, Sophie?"

With some effort, she tore her gaze away from Jonas and turned to Luca. Her prince's face was pinched, his blue eyes steely. "Uh," Sophie began unpromisingly. "I—"

"Sophie!" Desperation reflected in Luca's eyes as his fingers dug painfully into her waist. "You and I, we belong together.

We've spent every single night together for a year. How can you think of giving up now? You know what's been done to me before. What Pia did to Frederick. You don't want to do that, do you?"

Sophie soothed him instantly, "No, no, I don't. I'm dancing with you, after all." To Jonas, however, she said. "Just a few more hours. Then we'll sit down for coffee and talk." She had so many things to say to him.

But Jonas shook his head and stepped even closer. Tomas followed on his heels, and for the first time, Sophie saw the murderous look Jonas had described in the latter's eyes. "No! There's no way you'll finish dancing tonight."

"You have to finish dancing!" Luca stressed instantly, panic creeping into his voice. "If you don't, I'll succumb to the curse again. How many decades will I have to wait before someone takes pity on me? Centuries! Sophie, it's only a few more hours."

"He's lying!" Jonas hissed.

Confused, Sophie looked from Luca to him. She noticed her prince was gradually losing patience. They were probably wasting precious time talking.

"He would tell you anything just to get you to take the curse off him. But what he hasn't tell you is that afterwards, you'll take his place."

In one fell swoop, the club went silent. The monsters and demons around them looked ready to pounce on Jonas. Tomas had lost control over his face, almost frothing in anger. Sophie could see the other princes had also approached.

Uncertain, Sophie sought out Luca's gaze. "Is this true?" All feeling seemed to drain from her limbs.

"Of course it isn't. That's the biggest nonsense I've ever heard. It doesn't even make sense," Luca declared, rolling his eyes. The look he gave Jonas afterwards, however, made Sophie shudder. Searchingly, her fingers wandered to his arm, which still had a tight grip on her waist. Luca loosened his grip a little.

Jonas was not so quick to give in. "I heard it from one of them. A prince who was freed that way. It's true. When morning dawns, Luca will be a free man, and you'll have to dance down here forever." Pleadingly, Jonas looked at her. "You must believe me, Sophie!"

Everything in her resisted the notion. She didn't want to believe that the last year had been one giant lie. That she had only been a means to an end for Luca. At the same time, Sophie was aware that Jonas had never lied to her, no matter how uncomfortable the truth was for him. He had always been painfully honest. Even now, the fear and concern for her was predominant in his gaze.

Luca's fingers closed around Sophie's chin again and turned her face to him, so she was staring directly into his deep blue eyes. "Do you really think all of this hasn't been real? I love you, Sophie. You're the best thing that's ever happened to me."

Jonas snorted. "Yeah, because she'll get you out of this hell."

"He's right," a familiar voice suddenly spoke up. It was the woman who had tried to warn her once before.

"Sina!" With a quick step, Tomas reached the desperate woman. She, after all, he could hold on to. "Come! I'll make you something to drink."

The woman didn't manage to tear herself away from him, but her gaze sought out Sophie's. "It's all true! I gave him a year and a dance." Tomas dragged her along without care. Sina's face disappeared into the crowd, but her words still rang out. "No sooner was he free than I was trapped. Thirty years! For thirty years I've had to..." The rest was lost in a gurgle that made Sophie's heart beat faster.

Startled, she turned to Jonas who, like her, had been watching anxiously. His desperate gaze found Sophie's. "You can't let this happen, Sophie. Come with me! Trust me! Just this once," he pleaded.

Sophie had to swallow. Fear spread through her as she came to terms with the possibility that Sina and Jonas were right.

Luca must have noticed her change of heart, because instead of making more promises to her, he merely called out to his brother, "Play up, Bastien!"

The very first note went straight through her marrow. The music vibrated inside of Sophie and, as if of their own accord, her feet began to move. Helplessly, she reached out for Jonas, but Luca spun her around so fast that she lost all sight and hearing. The music became her everything. Only the dance had meaning. The melody flowed through her body and spurred her on. Luca mercilessly led her along under the dark battlements, lifted her high into the air, and making her perform the most complicated figures.

Her breath came in gasps and her heart beat violently in her chest, but Sophie couldn't escape the pull of the music. She tirelessly planted her feet, stretched and bent her body, slipped from splits into pirouettes and gave herself over to the music. She no longer knew what was happening around her. The sounds had banished all other noises. Someone reached for her, but the dance gave her no chance to see their face. She spun around until she came to rest in Lucas' arms.

His eyes shone as he leaned down. His kiss took her breath away and passion made her cheeks glow. Then the music demanded her attention again. Sophie gave it everything she had, regardless of the warning signals her body was sending. Her feet ached as if she were dancing on broken glass, and her head was spinning from all the rotations and jumps. Luca was the only constant in this wild dance.

Then, all at once, he let go of her, his eyes wide in horror. A blanket spread around her, soft as a cloud. It was the precious cloak Jonas had been wearing. It prevented Luca from touching her. Jonas, on the other hand, took her hand and implored her to leave. "Come now, Sophie! We don't have much time left." The demons were already creeping closer now that they'd sensed a weak spot.

Sophie realised she had lost all sense of time when she'd fallen under the spell of the music. She nodded, but once again, the melody caught her and her feet carried her to Luca, despite the cloak. Terrified, she dragged Jonas with her and tried to resist the dance, but it was as if she had lost control of her body.

Luca was waiting for her. The smile on his lips frightened her. Gone was his loving gaze, replaced by a cruelty.

"The shoes, Sophie. It's the shoes!" shouted Jonas behind her, still trying to pull her away from Luca. More and more desperation mixed into his voice. "The shoes tie you to The DeModie. That's why you couldn't leave them behind. Remember the nail in the wall!"

The words didn't make sense. She'd never seen the wall with the shoes, didn't even know if it existed. How could her shoes be cursed? They were her mother's much-loved shoes, after all. "That's not possible."

The pain on Jonas' face almost broke her heart. "Yes, it is. You've only ever worn them. No matter what happened. Even in the rain and snow. But they've been broken for a long time."

"But they're my mother's," Sophie countered, feeling herself slipping away from Jonas because her feet had other plans for her. She had to dance. Had to dance with Luca, whether she wanted to or not.

One more time, Jonas grabbed her and pulled her from the beat again. "Let her go already, Sophie! The shoes aren't your mother. They won't bring her back to you. You have to let them go." Suddenly, a demon lunged at Jonas and yanked him away by the shoulders. Horrified, Sophie watched the monster forcibly take the red life energy from him. The same kind of energy she'd already given so many of them.

"Now come on." Luca's gentle words soothed her nerves. He was reaching for her. Despite the cloak around her shoulders, her feet carried her towards him.

Behind her, Jonas cried out in pain, and the sound made Sophie shiver. Intimidated, she looked at Luca, whose smile was widening. He knew she couldn't escape him.

At last, Sophie found her defiance. Leaning forward, she tugged the frayed ribbons apart.

"Sophie, don't!" warned Luca, panic returning to his voice.

Spurred on by his reaction, Sophie tore the first shoe off her foot. Broken as it was, it almost fell apart upon her rough handling. The sound of the ripping fabric broke her heart, and hot tears ran down her cheeks. The second shoe followed, and Sophie threw the pair into Luca's horrified face. "There you go. This is what you wanted after all," she cried, finally turning away from the prince.

Panicked, Sophie's gaze flitted through the crowd in search of Jonas. Relieved, she found him still standing. Holding a silver branch in one hand and a gold branch in the other, he was fighting for his life. To her amazement, the monsters dodged the branches as if they were afraid of the touch.

With a kick, Jonas transported a wolf-like creature back into the crowd, knocking down two creatures with long claws in the process. Still, the demons managed to feed on his life energy again and again.

Sophie had no idea how long Jonas could withstand the assault. After all, he was still suffering from his terrible memories and might not have as much life force as she'd once possessed. Luca's moaning behind her, however, reminded her of the danger she was in.

Spurred on by the threat, she pushed her way through the crowd that was backing away from the coat and grabbed Jonas by the elbow. For one maddening moment, he set to strike, and her heart beat violently in her chest. She had seen that look on his face before: the naked fear that made him lash out wildly. But Jonas recognised her and grabbed her hand as he made a breach for them with the branches. "Let's get out of here!"

Together, they fled from Luca, who roared behind her, "Make way, you freaks!"

Her body ached from the exertion of the last year, and her mind was tired. If Jonas hadn't been tirelessly pulling her along, Sophie would have never tried to escape.

The music still boomed in her ears for a little longer, then it ended with a bang. Suddenly, the ground gave way beneath them, and cold water welcomed them. The dance floor had turned into the lake it represented. Panic took hold of Sophie. She clung to Jonas in her desperation. He had dropped the branches and was swimming towards one of the boats instead. It was only a few metres away, but the distance proved challenging all the same.

The monsters were trapped on shore, if they hadn't been unlucky enough to fall into the water themselves. But lost souls in the water reached for them with pale hands. Their swollen faces displayed the terror she felt, their mouths open in silent screams. They reached for Jonas and threatened to pull him into the depths, whereas the cloak protected Sophie even here. It didn't even soak with water, instead floating like a cloud on the surface. Without further ado, Sophie grabbed the fabric and pulled it around Jonas' shoulder as well, giving him a much-needed respite.

Shortly afterwards, they reached the boat and Jonas helped Sophie climb in. The boat tilted dangerously towards her, then she was inside and crouched on the floor, panting. It rocked violently once more, until Jonas had also pulled himself over the edge, knocking at least three pairs of hands off himself. Out of breath, he checked on Sophie, then leaned back for a moment. Trembling, Sophie wrapped her arms around her body.

A shadow flew over them, destroying their brief moment of calm. Jonas sat up and looked around the boat that had once been a sitting area. Water sloshed against the wood.

"What are we going to do now?" Sophie asked once she'd caught her breath. Completely soaked, she was freezing miserably.

Jonas raised his index finger to his lips, and Sophie fell silent. She racked her brain for a solution, but the cold didn't allow her to think clearly. At last, with a few practised moves, Jonas broke the small table in half so he could use the table leg as a misshapen paddle.

Unable to help him, Sophie huddled in the bow and faced the shore. Jonas's paddle was not particularly effective, but it brought them closer to the forest of gold and silver inch by inch.

The shore wasn't deserted. Most of the monsters had stayed by the castle, but some had made it to the other side of the lake. Among them stood a tall figure she knew better than any other. Luca was blocking the stairs. Two pitch-black, leathery wings spread across his back.

"So, it was his shadow," Sophie stated, shuddering as she recognised the shoes Luca held out in his hand.

"Hmm?" Jonas looked past her now too and cursed loudly. "He's bloody persistent! Don't worry, Sophie, there's no way I'm going to let him have you." His brave words gave her little hope. Sophie couldn't see how she'd ever escape from this club.

Jonas left the boat to the waves, which carried them the last few metres towards the shore, and stood up, his self-made paddle in his hand like a baseball bat.

Luca grinned before calling out, "She's mine, Jonas! She committed herself to The DeModie a long time ago. Your pathetic rebellion won't change that. It's too late. The year and the day are up."

Sophie almost threw up. The prospect of spending her whole life down here took her breath away.

Jonas was less impressed as he jumped off the boat onto the bejewelled beach. "Oh yeah? Then why aren't you out in the sun enjoying your freedom?"

Luca hissed, his face contorting into an ugly grimace. He jumped at Jonas, who hit him across the face with the wood.

Startled, Sophie cried out and put her hands over her mouth.

Dazed, Luca staggered to the side and Jonas reached out a hand to help her out of the boat. As if in a trance, she stumbled out and watched Luca wipe some blood from the corner of his mouth. Underneath, his face was flawless. His blue eyes sparkled.

"Watch out!" she shouted to Jonas in a panic.

Jonas whirled around and knocked Luca's arm aside. The ugly cracking noise didn't seem to bother Luca much. Instead, he grabbed the log and held it motionless in the air while Jonas struggled to jerk the makeshift weapon from his grasp.

On a quick decision, Sophie bent down and threw a handful of the precious stones into Luca's face.

Surprised, the demon prince let go. At the same moment, Jonas hit him in the ribs with the heavy wood. Gasping, Luca stumbled backwards.

Jonas, however, flung the table leg away and grabbed Sophie's hand once more. He fled with her past the monsters through the forest. Luca pursued them mercilessly, closely followed by the other monsters.

The delicate moss splintered under their heavy footfall, and Sophie felt as if she were walking on a thousand shards. However, the cries of pain that suddenly rang out weren't hers. They both stopped in horror.

Luca's face was contorted, and he gasped, pausing for a moment. Had the blows caused more damage than she'd previously thought?

For a moment, Sophie was tempted to check on him. She'd loved Luca for a year. When their eyes met, however, she could no longer recognise her lover. Hatred blazed in his eyes and his face resembled more of a horrifying mask.

Panic gripped Sophie again, and she squeezed Jonas' hand, so that he would move on. But then she noticed that Jonas' eyes were wide open and staring into the distance.

"Jonas!" she groaned in horror. "Now is not the time to have another attack. Come on!"

He didn't move.

Instead, Luca came closer and closer. "A fine hero you've chosen, Sophie." Mockery curled his lips despite the scratches on his neck.

Scratches.

All at once, Sophie remembered the evenings on which Jonas must have broken off the branches. There had been loud thunder, and then another scratch had appeared on Luca or he'd twisted his foot. That was why the twigs had also served Jonas as weapons against the monsters in his desperate struggle.

Resolutely, Sophie grabbed the nearest branch and broke it off, her eyes fixed on Luca.

He sank to the ground, cursing and holding his side. The familiar thunder rang through the leaves and sent them jangling, and all at once, Jonas gasped. His eyes were clear again.

"Break off as much of the trees' branches as you can," Sophie instructed Jonas, seeing how Luca got back to his feet out of the corner of her eye. "It's hurting him." At last, she understood. Everything in The DeModie was connected.

Jonas didn't ask for an explanation, but hastily dragged her on. Without consideration, they trampled over the moss and broke branches from the trees left and right.

It wasn't just Luca and his henchmen who suffered. The illusion of beauty also vanished. Dark storm clouds hung in the sky below a shimmering red cave wall. The water of the lake was pitch black and surged in the darkness. Monsters and lost souls lurked on the shores, reaching out to them in everlasting hunger. With time, the glittering forest turned into a dead landscape of horror.

Luca was still pursuing them, but he had slowed down. Others had taken up the chase instead. There were huffs and puffs beside and behind them. Something ran through the forest, making the whole ground shake and the shards of glass clink. Shadows flew over them and Sophie wished she had somewhere to hide, but there was no such hiding place in the forest with its delicate limbed trees. Besides, giving up was no longer an option.

Thick tears obscured her vision. She had long since lost track of where they were and where they had to go to escape this nightmare. Luca cried out for her, but his voice sounded distorted and caused her to shiver. Only Jonas' grip on her hand gave her hope. As long as he guided her, she couldn't be lost.

Just then, Jonas came to a stop. "No, no, no," he whispered.

Sophie hardly dared to take a look, but by then, she saw what had made him stop. In front of her, a wall full of broken shoes stretched, and at the very end hung her mother's pointe shoes. Her heart was in her throat, since she had no idea how they'd got there. Luca had only just been holding them in his hand. Whimpering, she looked at the shoes she had loved so much and which had been her downfall.

"It's too late," she heard herself moan.

Jonas shook his head with a passion. "No, the sun isn't in the sky yet." He looked at his watch and nodded, his words confirmed. Then he grabbed her hand again. "But now I know where we have to go."

Together they ran on into the darkness. The door appeared in front of them, and Sophie exhaled in relief. There was no sign of Luca. Relief spread through her. They would actually make it, shoes or no shoes.

Something crashed into Jonas and tore them apart. Her coat caught in the claws of leathery wings that brushed against her for a moment. It was pulled from her shoulders as the creature and Jonas tumbled down the steps. Horrified, Sophie recognised the demon's face as he sat on Jonas and closed his hands around his neck.

Tomas.

He had always been the dearest of the brothers after Luca to her, kind and obliging, often more concerned about her than Luca himself. She still remembered how he had refused to mix her more potent drinks. Or his scowl when Luca had got his way, regardless. Now he was no different from the others. Like them, Tomas was nothing more than a gruesome monster, with only murder on his mind.

And Jonas had been right: Tomas wanted to kill him.

Startled, Sophie watched, unable even to move.

Still a little stunned by the impact, Jonas reached for the hands around his neck, brought his knee up, and rammed it into Tomas' groin. At the same moment, Jonas hit Tomas' forearms while he was still writhing. The hands came loose, and Jonas attacked again. The military training kicked in, but

Tomas possessed the same supernatural strength that Luca had displayed. The blows hardly bothered him.

"Run, Sophie! Get out of here!" Jonas shouted at her, before Tomas smashed his face into the steps.

She could no longer tell which of the two had the upper hand, only heard bones crunching and skin slapping against skin. Sophie didn't want to leave Jonas behind, not in this predicament, but she couldn't let his sacrifice be in vain either. With some effort, she tore her eyes from their sight and rushed towards the door, only to find that Luca had beaten her to it.

He was standing there, smiling. Wings resting on his back, he held out his hand to her. Whimpering, Sophie backed away. But then he was with her, pressing her to him. No sooner had he touched her than the music filled her ears, as if it had only been waiting for this moment. Although she resisted his guidance and her feet were no longer in the cursed shoes, it was easy for Luca to make her dance. Every attempt of hers to get to the door became an expressive movement of her body. If she tried to jump away, he lifted her and pulled her back again, and each time, they moved further away from the door.

Sophie cried out in exasperation. She was so close and yet so far.

Luca acknowledged her distress with a smile, bent down and whispered harshly against the crook of her neck, "It's too late, Sophie. You will set me free."

"No, she won't." A new voice had joined the fray. "It's not your turn."

Sophie almost didn't recognise him, but when he grabbed her and lifted her up, she realised it was Frederick, Luca's older brother. His eyes were bloodshot and his movements rough and violent.

Gasping, Sophie twisted in his arms before Luca demanded her back. "Give it up already! The last dance is mine," he hissed at his older brother. His grip also hurt Sophie, and she felt herself being thrown around, rather more like a doll than a dancer. "Dance, Sophie! Dance!"

The music whipped her into motion. Her feet were on fire. Her pulse was pounding. Everything inside her seemed to be turned outside, pushed away from her by an unknown force. Red streaks formed around her and disappeared into the darkness. With each turn, the music bound her to it. To The DeModie.

All of a sudden, Sophie spun free and stumbled away from Luca. But it wasn't because the night was over, and he had gained freedom. Frederick still hadn't admitted defeat. Instead of Sophie, he now held down Luca, unwilling to let his younger brother have his victory.

"Sophie!" The demon prince reached out to her in desperation. Exhausted, Sophie stumbled against the wall behind her. Her knees went weak, and the floor seemed to come towards her.

No!

She couldn't give up now, not after everything that had happened. She cast her eyes around for Jonas and discovered him lying lifeless on the stairs. There was no sign of Tomas.

With a cry of horror, Sophie rushed towards him and almost collapsed in relief when he stirred with a groan. Coughing, Jonas rolled onto his knees and Sophie could see that blood had stained his hair a rusty brown.

A glance backwards told her that she didn't have much time left. But she couldn't leave Jonas here. Not after all he'd done for her and not with all that she felt for him. Determined, she reached under his arms and pulled him to his feet. He was leaning on her much heavier than she'd anticipated, but the adrenaline helped her withstand his weight.

"It's not far," Sophie whispered, eliciting an almost delirious smile from him. At the sight, icy fingers of fear pierced her heart. "Please don't give up now."

Her words must have reached him as, suddenly, Jonas straightened up and grabbed her by the waist. "He's coming."

Swallowing, Sophie realised he spoke the truth.

Luca had freed himself from Frederick's grip and was charging forward, his face contorted with anger. "Don't you dare, Sophie! Don't you dare do this to me!"

She ignored him. Together, she and Jonas exerted the last of their strength and rushed towards the door. Jonas yanked on the handle so hard it fell into his hand. Fresh, cold night air hit them in the face.

Now there was only terrible fear in Luca's eyes. He had almost reached them when Sophie stepped out into the open and pulled Jonas with her.

The door slammed shut, and with a thunderous roar, the club began to fall apart. The neon sign came crashing down and a long crack raced from the roof through the door. Stone crumbled and dust trickled down on them.

In horror, Jonas and Sophie backed away. Without taking his eyes off the club, Jonas pressed Sophie against him, and she wrapped her arms around his waist. Together, they stared at the crumbling building, which was slowly sinking into a crevice in the earth. The top had only just disappeared when the two buildings next to it moved together with a jolt.

The terror was over.

Not a breath of air stirred. There was an almost eerie silence after the noise in The DeModie. Not a single piece of the club had remained. Even the dust had settled. Sophie swallowed as she slowly began to understand the horror they had barely escaped.

As the soft dawn appeared in the sky, her pulse calmed, and she caught her breath. Jonas turned to her and exhaled in relief. Blood from a cut was stuck to his forehead and in his hair. His face was already turning blue in places, but he was grinning wider by the second.

"We did it."

All at once, he hugged Sophie tightly and kissed her on the forehead.

Tears came to her eyes, but they were tears of joy and relief. She was insanely happy they had both escaped safely from The DeModie.

Jonas let go of her again. He regarded Sophie with a loving gaze and wiped the tears from her cheeks. Then he held out his hand to her. "You promised me a coffee, I believe."

With a smile, she placed her hand in his. The night chill seeped into her bare feet as she snuggled against him again. They still ached from the year-long ordeal, but Sophie didn't care. For the first time in a year, she felt free.

Prima Ballerina

"I think they're ready soon." Jonas was almost more excited than she was. Even though this wasn't even about him.

Sophie shook her head with a grin and stood next to him, one leg raised high above her head as she stretched.

In front of the stage, the examiners took their seats. Next to her, the other girls went through their routines again. Sophie would be the first to perform, and slowly, she was getting nervous, too. She'd rehearsed for months after the prescribed medical rest for her feet had expired. Now they were in pointe shoes again. But this time, they were her own shoes. The ones she had bought with Jonas. They fit like a glove, and her feet finally felt whole again.

The pianist played a few notes as a test and then looked at the sheets again.

Sophie looked up at Jonas with a smile. "Weren't you planning to study for your exam?"

Jonas snorted. "As if I could while you have your audition. You'll back out if I'm not here."

Sophie nudged his side. "I wouldn't." The hall started to quiet down.

"I believe in you, Sophie," he suddenly said, all sombre, resting his forehead against hers.

"I know." He always had, but now she did so as well. "I'm ready," she promised.

Jonas smiled. "Good."

"Sophie Kallenbach," a voice called. All at once, the excitement multiplied a hundredfold. She hadn't been on stage for so long and wasn't yet ready to undergo such critical scrutiny.

Jonas pulled her close once more. "You can do it." Then she felt his lips on hers, and for a moment, the world stood still as his confidence filled her. The kiss was far too short, but time was of the essence. "Break a leg!"

Sophie laughed and hurried up the steps. Before she stepped out, her face was smooth again. Chin raised, fingers stretched to their tips, she stepped onto the stage with a springy step. The spotlight blinded her to the reviewers, but the wood beneath her pointed the way. Calm settled over her as she took her position. Her body awaited the dance, the steps firmly burned into her memory. Every nerve was stretched to the utmost, ready to surrender to the music. Her feet yearned to move, and Sophie could hardly wait to give in to her desire.

Like a light summer rain, the first notes fell into her lap, and a slight smile stole onto her lips. She was home. The music was hers again.

Join the Story Seekers

Want to read more?

If you liked this book and want to read more, try out the Spirit Seeker series. Subscribers to my Story Seeker Newsletter will get the Spirit Seeker Prequel Natural Selection for free plus behind-the-scenes, extra scenes, and book deals. Always stay on top of magical news from Janna Ruth. Sign up at https://www.janna-ruth.com/newsletter

Please review!

Authors depend on reviews to get the word out about their books. If you enjoyed Ashuan, consider reviewing it on Amazon or Goodreads or your personal blog.

Want some fun?

If you want to chat with me and other readers about my various books, join my Facebook group via https://www.facebook.com/authorjannaruth. We will read together, discuss details, and have some fun with games and giveaways.

**I'm a ghost whisperer, not a catacomb crawler. But when
you live in Paris, sometimes you end up being both.**

·

Hi, I'm Alix. During the day, I'm a history student at the
time-honoured Sorbonne University. After class, I hang out
with the ghosts of the revolution, the many undead misunder-
stood Parisian artists, and adventurous scientists that glow in
the dark. None of them are alive, but they come to me to solve
their problems with the living.

When a recently deceased catacomb tour guide asks me to
retrieve a mysterious personal item from the underground,
things take a turn for the weird. Suddenly, I find myself in a city
of ghosts, hunted by murderous cave crawlers, and stumbling
across haunting secrets.

If I'm not careful now, I might end up a ghost myself.

·

**Urban Fantasy with a French twist. If you like cave-crawl-
ing adventures, hopeless romantics, and ghosts, you'll enjoy Ghosts of the Catacombs, the first book of the Parisian
Ghosts series. Travel to Paris today to embark on your
catacomb adventure.**

JANNA RUTH

GHOSTS
OF THE
CATACOMBS

PARISIAN GHOSTS 1

About Janna Ruth

Janna Ruth made her self-publishing debut on June 13, 2017. Now, five years later, her award-winning fairy-tale retelling "Melody of a Curse" (OT: Im Bann der zertanzten Schuhe) is finally available in English. Since then, Janna has built an impressive backlist of Urban Fantasy series, fairy-tale retellings, and coming-of-age adventures in both German and English. When she isn't working on one of her books, she's decorating cakes, running after her three boys, or picking up a new craft-project that will forever be unfinished.

For more books by Janna Ruth, visit

www.janna-ruth.com